TARA NINA

The Cursed MacKinnons

Dual Release

A Sensual Erotic Romance

DUAL RELEASE

CURSED MACKINNONS SERIES

BOOK 5

BY

Tara Nina

Dual Release

Please be advised this book was previously published in 2014.

It has been revised prior to current release.

All rights reserved
Copyright© 2019 by Tara Nina
Cover Art by Syneca of OriginalSyn
Published by T.N.Books

ISBN

ebook: 9781734205787

Print: 9781734205794

To obtain permission to excerpt portions of the text, please contact the author at

http://taranina.com

T.N.Books
New Jersey
2018

Published in the USA

Thank you for purchasing this novel.

It's the support & love of the readers,

And my family,

That makes my world a better place.

Tara Nina

Dedication

This novel is dedicated to my Sizzling Scribe Sister, Cait Miller. She has been tremendously helpful with her extensive knowledge of Scotland (considering she lives there, it's a plus).

Acknowledgments

As always, I wouldn't be anywhere in this world if it wasn't for the love of my family. These books wouldn't even exist if it wasn't for the help of my dearest and closest friends: Colleen, Kim, Cait, Jen, & Lynn. Y'all are the world's greatest sounding boards for crazy ideas.

Chapter One

Guarded by a tortured soul
A widowed mistress coddles thy
  brathairs paired
Indebted by unfortunate fates
Their future waits
Hidden beneath wooden planks
Lies stairs o' blood
Safely they be swathed 'n Fraser green

The translated version of the riddle of the twins rolled through her thoughts as she steadily walked the streets of London. Belvedere tugged happily on his leash, leading as if he knew the way. It had taken months to decipher the riddle that eventually led them to Fraser Castle. Chills skittered down her spine at the memory of standing in the "Green Room" at the top of the once supposedly bloodstained stairs.

As she stood in that room, the words *they were here* floated in the air. When the ghost of a young woman appeared, May knew the whispered rumors about a princess being murdered there were true. The specter's sad eyes still lingered in her mind. Something bad happened to that young woman, but for now it remained a mystery. May's main focus was on freeing the remaining MacKinnon brothers.

The clues led to Fraser Castle, which in turn pointed them to The Hunterian Museum where many of the castle's artifacts had been donated in the early fifties. The museum reported several years prior the "sleeping twins" statue, as they called it, was sold to a buyer who wished to remain anonymous. Not even an offer of a substantial donation to their cause could loosen their lips.

If she hadn't by chance seen a picture in the paper… She took a deep breath. What if she was wrong? May took a moment at the corner across from the newly built art gallery. Was she hoping against hope she'd found them? She turned and fidgeted with her hair as she stared at her reflection in a storefront window. Out of the corner of her eye, she thought she saw something odd. Knowing danger lurked, waiting to strike the brothers, kept her alert to strange things that stood out from the normal.

Casually she tilted her chin, acting as if she fussed with her appearance but focused on a man in a trench coat. Was he following her? Had she seen him a couple blocks back when she'd stopped to allow Belvedere a few minutes in a dog park? He entered a store and she breathed a sigh of relief. Overactive imagination playing tricks, but then again it could be pointing out a possible threat. For several seconds, she studied the door where the man disappeared. He didn't come right back out so she had to be wrong. He wasn't following her. She shook her head and turned to the crosswalk.

Now was as good a time as any to determine if her hunch was correct. Was she ready to face *him*? It had been years. Did something still exist between them? Her heart skipped a beat. The light changed and she stepped off the curb and walked along with the rest of the crowd across the street.

She admired the well-manicured garden gracing the front of the gallery. A small outdoor bistro was to the right of the door with tables and chairs placed under umbrellas on the lawn. A few stone benches lined the walkways weaving through the trees, shrubs and flowers. It gave a welcoming appeal to the uniquely round building with black glass walls.

People were scattered about, enjoying the weeklong grand-opening event. At the top of the stairs, her hand froze on the gallery's door handle. Was it excitement at seeing an old friend again churning her stomach into a buttery mess? Or was the fear of being wrong about the twins' location making her hesitate?

May breathed deeply as she looked at her sidekick, who sat patiently waiting with his tongue sticking out to the side and big brown eyes staring at her. She smiled. "You're right, Belvedere. Time to pull up my big-girl panties and get this done."

* * * * *

Jameson knew the name of his surprise visitor before he even looked up from his work. He heard the soft swish of silk, the jingle of her bracelets and inhaled the scent of her perfume, an essence he'd never forget along with the woman. May Allison Kenly-Wentworth-Breckenridge, the woman he'd let slip through his fingers *twice*.

He lifted his gaze from the invoice and focused on her. His heart beat faster. Her hair was no longer bright red but a lighter shade, more auburn with gray streaks, which only added to her character. She wore it in a loose bun on top of her head with several strands dangling free, outlining her angelic face. It made him smile to see the sexy freckles still spattered across her cute button nose. Even though many years had passed, her wondrous green eyes shone bright with the excitement of a child at Christmas.

Her outfit was typical May. No matter how much money she had in her bank account, she followed no fashion trend. She set her own. Today wasn't any different. He loved the bold-colored dress, but wished it didn't fit so loosely, hiding what he imagined was a perfect womanly body.

Strutting on a leash at her side was the cutest dog he'd seen in a while. Being unfamiliar with dogs, he couldn't guess the breed, but it was a lovely shade of brown and white, with fluffy ears and a cropped tail. Unbelievably, it had brown freckles across the bridge of its white snout.

He rolled his wheelchair from behind his desk and headed in her direction.

"May, what a wonderful surprise."

She reached for his outstretched hand as she crossed the room and met him halfway. He hadn't changed. He still looked delectable even with the scattered shades of gray peppering his wavy black hair. When he leveled those deep-blue eyes on her, she swore her knees wobbled. Yep. He still had the magic to make her tingle with a look.

"Jameson Archer, you haven't changed a bit," May stated exuberantly.

"You have, May. You've gotten even more beautiful than I remember." He lifted her hand to his lips and pressed a tender kiss to the back of it. May was thankful she'd chosen the loose-fitting, silk kimono-styled dress. If she'd worn something form-fitting, he'd know the effect he had on her by the sudden hardness of her nipples. She blinked, trying to force her focus from his perfect set of lips.

Belvedere barked a warning the moment Jameson's lips made contact with her skin. May petted his head to soothe his angst, but it didn't keep him from positioning himself between her and Jameson's wheelchair.

"Thank you, Jameson. Still the sweet talker I remember." She grinned.

Her many bracelets jingled when he fingered the charms that dangled from one of them. He caught the sterling silver unicorn, rubbing it between his forefinger and thumb. "I'm amazed to see you've still got this one."

"I take good care of my most prized possessions."

"This is one of them?" he questioned.

"Of course," she replied, gently tugging her hand free. "One of my dearest and oldest friends gave it to me."

"Ah." He laughed. "Now I'm old."

"As am I," May retorted as she touched his shoulder playfully. She couldn't help but note the strength she felt beneath her palm. All that upper-body muscle…

"No, May. You are timeless."

Before she thought better of it, candid words exited her mouth. "Tell that to the wrinkles in the corners of my eyes and my sagging ass."

Jameson burst out laughing. His infectiously rich laughter made her join in. When they both regained their composure, he motioned for her to sit on the couch.

Belvedere stuck to her side and took a protective stance between them. He gave another low yip of warning as if claiming May as his and never took his eyes off Jameson.

"I see you have a new champion of sorts. What's his name?"

"Belvedere. He's an English Springer Spaniel and quite protective."

Jameson offered Belvedere his hand to smell and decide whether Jameson was friend or foe. After a few seconds, the pup licked him and allowed Jameson to stroke behind his ear.

"You keep doing that and he'll be in your lap," May pointed out.

"I don't think I'd mind at all." Jameson smiled as he wagged his eyebrows. "It's been a while since I've had anything warm and cozy in my lap."

May rolled her eyes and shook her head as she replied, "You are incorrigible."

"You wouldn't have me any other way," he declared teasingly. "Would you care for a drink?"

"A cup of tea would be nice."

"Not a problem." He smiled, rolled over to his desk, pressed a button on the phone and requested afternoon tea and snacks be brought in for his guest. Jameson maneuvered his wheelchair so he faced May across the coffee table. "What brings you to London? How did you know I was here?"

"Jameson, you never do anything small. The opening of your latest art gallery has been posted in every paper from here to New York. How could I not know where to find you?"

"Why, pray tell, lovely lady, have you been looking for me?"

Was that a hint of lust she saw in his eyes? It couldn't be. Jameson was her oldest and dearest friend. She couldn't help but remember he and her first husband were best friends. Did he somehow know she'd fallen in love with both of them? Nah, she decided. That was a secret she'd kept to herself. When Hal died, Jameson had been there to help her through that dark time. As her friend, he'd supported her. Nothing more. Could it have been more if he hadn't been married to Muriel?

Though she tried to stop the rapid train of thought, it proceeded. By the time he divorced Muriel, she'd already married her second husband, Stanley. It just never seemed to be the right opportunity for them. She attempted to stop reasoning the why behind their not being together. Looking at him now, she couldn't help but wonder what it would've been like if things happened the other way around in her first marriage.

If she'd married Jameson instead of Hal. She shook the what-could've-been scenario from her thoughts. That was many years and two husbands ago.

May tried to turn her thoughts away from the tenderness she felt for Jameson, but the caress of his gaze refused to let her. Could there be something romantic left between them? Unfortunately there was this little bit of business she needed to take care of before anything else could take precedence in her life. She shooed away the fantasy of romance and got down to the reason for her visit.

"I have to admit I've been looking for you, Jameson." She settled into the corner of the comfy couch. Belvedere snuggled close to her side as she absently rubbed his coat. "Your latest collection has a couple of items I am interested in purchasing."

"And here I thought you'd come to see me." He gave her a playful pout, but it disappeared immediately when there was a tap at the door a second before Jameson's assistant LaVerne opened it and pushed in a cart with a tray of cookies, a silver teapot, a wooden box filled with assorted teas, two teacups on saucers with napkins and matching silver teaspoons. And just for Belvedere, there was a clear glass bowl containing water. Belvedere hopped down and sat patiently waiting, as if everything on the tray were for him.

"Will that be all, sir?" LaVerne asked in a nasal English accent. May couldn't help but admire the well-dressed, slender man with perfectly coiffed, snow-white hair and black-rimmed glasses. She liked the way he treated Belvedere as he placed the dish on the floor in front of him and stroked his fur.

"Yes. Thank you, LaVerne."

He nodded in Jameson's direction as he stood and left.

Jameson lifted the silver teapot and poured hot water into both cups as she selected a teabag. Once the tea was prepared, she sat back, took a sip and watched him over the rim of her cup. Tea was something she'd never seen him drink. Brandy, Irish whiskey, an occasional beer but never hot tea. Odd she remembered something like that. A slight smile tickled her lips. He sipped his then started the conversation again.

"Which items interested you, my dear?"

May set her cup on the table and pulled a folded newspaper article out of the pocket of her dress. Unfolding it, she handed it to him. For a moment he studied the wrinkled piece of paper. Peering over its upper edge, he gave her a perplexed look as he said, "This is just a picture of me outside the warehouse watching the crew unload crates. There's nothing here but me." His grin broadened. "Dare I hope the item of which you speak *is* me?"

Heat flushed her cheeks for the first time in many years. She usually held her own with the men in her life, but Jameson always had a way of making her blush. When she found her voice, she couldn't believe how husky it sounded in response to his teasing. "In time, dear Jameson, we can research that possibility."

She stood and moved around the table to his side, holding his ardent gaze. She didn't blink, afraid that what she hoped she saw wouldn't be there when her vision cleared. After all these years, was there a chance she and Jameson could be more than friends? May took a steadying breath. She leaned until they were nearly cheek-to-cheek and then pointed to an open crate inside the warehouse.

It seemed like the heat of his gaze caressed her finger as it traversed its length to locate the item to which she pointed. He squinted, then leaned back. A broad grin brightened his face as he looked at her.

"That's one of my most prized possessions. Not sure I can part with it."

May settled onto the arm of his wheelchair and rested her arm around his shoulders. She flashed him her best wide-eyed innocent look, while cupping his chin in her other hand. "I'm really interested in that particular piece. Name your price."

Pure heat seared her insides from the drop-dead, sexy look he pierced her with as his voice lowered. "You."

She leaned back, staring at him. Doing her best not to show how much his words threw her business manner into a tailspin, she said, "I'm not so sure that's a fair price. These statues are far more valuable than I."

LaVerne buzzed in through the phone's intercom and startled May, who jumped to a standing position. "Mr. Archer, the gentlemen from the auction house are here."

Jameson rolled over to the desk, pressed a button and replied, "Tell them I'll be with them in a few moments." He turned to May and smiled. "I'm sorry but I need to speak with them. We've been trying to set a date and time to sell a few pieces, but it's been a phone-tag game this week."

"Please tell me you're not placing the statues of the twins on the block."

"That depends on you," he teased with a wag of his eyebrows and she couldn't help but laugh. He reached for her hand. "Have dinner with me tonight and I'll keep them off the auction list."

"Jameson," she replied. "How could I refuse an offer like that?"

Chapter Two

Cait sat brooding over the events of her day. She'd had a late night at the pub, which led to a hot tip for an article. The man she'd met rambled on and on about a strange brotherhood. He wouldn't have caught her attention so much if she hadn't read a snippet on the Internet about that same brotherhood. She couldn't believe her luck. Though the tidbit of information disappeared, it had piqued her interest and she hadn't been able to forget about it for months.

According to her dear old Gran, everything happened for a reason. That man taking a seat beside her and pouring out his heart over his so-called stupid assignment was a sign she was supposed to find and expose this demonic brotherhood to the paranormal world through her online magazine. At least that's what she believed. If her Gran had been sitting in that bar with her, she would've told her to follow her instinct on the issue and run with it.

Yawning, she battled the threat of fatigue. Right about now there wasn't an ounce of her willing to run anywhere. She'd followed him from the bar. When he parked his car outside a hotel, she did the same. At first she was worried he might notice her even though she'd kept several parked cars between them. She'd relaxed the moment he laid his seat back and it appeared as if he passed out. Making sure to keep Jenny, her partner, abreast of her whereabouts, she'd called.

Early that morning, Jenny had met her where she'd been parked all night. The man hadn't moved, which was tough on Cait's spirit. It had been a long night of touch-and-gos trying to stay awake. Without a decent cup of tea, it was a damnable feat of strength not to have fallen asleep. Cait blew across the rim of the Styrofoam cup Jenny had brought her. The first sip soothed a smidgeon of her discomfort, but it had taken the whole cup to keep her eyes open.

Mid-morning finally brought them some action and had them doing a steady walk to keep up as he followed a woman when she left the hotel. She had a dog on a leash and set a decent pace. When they finally entered an art exhibit, it was a bit of a break Cait needed to catch a rest.

"You wouldn't be so winded if you'd jog with me once in a while," Jenny teased in a hushed tone. Cait rolled her eyes in response. Jenny was always trying to get her to eat healthier and jog. With those long legs of hers, Jenny had no trouble keeping up, but Cait's steps were two to her one, since she was a bit on the shorter side.

"It's lack of sleep," Cait responded with a playful sneer. "Not exercise—or lack thereof—that's slowing me down today."

Together, she and Jenny surveyed the event while keeping their suspect in sight. It didn't take long before he was escorted to the door. From what they discerned, it seemed as if he'd gone down a hallway he shouldn't have been in. One at a time, they followed him out. He settled on a bench in a corner of the garden and watched the front door.

She and Jenny took seats at a table in the outdoor bistro area where they could still see him. They ordered tea and scones in an effort to look casual. No amount of tea would ease the questions plaguing her about this man. It bothered her that he seemed bent on tailing the older redheaded woman.

Was she his assignment? More importantly, what did she have that this brotherhood wanted? She and Jenny debated it, trying to figure out that one. The little bit of information she'd read was an open call for individuals with magical abilities to join the brotherhood. That had captured her interest but when she went back to the site to study it more, the website was gone. So now here she was, following a hunch.

Was the woman a witch? She nearly snorted a sip of her tea over that thought. If she was, wouldn't this "magical" brotherhood have approached her to join instead of followed her? Perhaps they had and she declined their offer and now they were after her for some mystical property in her possession. Cait pinched the bridge of her nose, doing her best to squelch the onslaught of ridiculous theories her extreme tiredness conjured. Jenny's hand on her arm made her meet her best friend's concerned gaze.

"Are you okay?"

"Yeah," Cait replied, then smiled. "The night's catching up with me, that's all."

"It's understandable. Would you like another cup of tea?"

"Yeah, but I don't think we've got time." She nodded toward the stairs at the sight of the redhead descending with the cute dog in tow.

When the redhead strolled down the walkway toward the street, their suspect eased from his hidden position and was on her trail again. They spent the rest of the day tailing him as he kept after her. It didn't make sense. Was he plotting her kidnapping? Or perhaps he planned to take her dog and hold it for ransom? Weird scenarios built in Cait's brain as she battled the desire to sleep. By the time late afternoon rolled around, they were back at the hotel. Jenny gave her a break and kept watch while she took a nap. Evening came and they were hot on his tail again as they sat outside a posh restaurant overlooking the Thames River.

Cait prayed she hadn't made a mistake as they watched the man in the car several spaces ahead of them. Since she and Jenny had been grabbing quick bites here and there while on surveillance, the delicious smells wafting from the restaurant were killing her.

"I hope we're not wasting our time watching this idiot." Jenny broke the silence in her soft Southern drawl. Cait loved to listen to her accent except when she was mad. Jenny felt the same way about her Scottish lilt. Apparently when *she* got angry the brogue thickened and *she* became harder to understand. Like Jenny didn't?

"So far he's the best lead we've had on this so-called Brotherhood of the Sons of the Servant of Judgment."

"From what you've said about him, he doesn't seem like he's that bright."

"His intelligence level isn't in question here. His connections are," Cait stated bluntly, then wished she hadn't. It had to be the lack of sleep making her snippy.

"Listen, Cait, I'm beginning to think that *tip* you got is a dead end. There is no such disturbed brotherhood recruiting members to help search for some dark book of magic spells," Jenny declared. She leaned catty-corner against the seat and the passenger door. In the dark, Cait could tell from Jenny's tone she was aggravated and if she could see Jenny's eyes, she knew they'd be glaring at her right now. It was a glare she'd experienced many times in their years together.

"I believe there is," Cait answered, forcing her tone to sound calm. She needed her cohort to stick with her on this one. "Is it not our job to investigate every strange tip thrown our way?"

"Yes," Jenny replied. "But this seems out there a bit more than usual."

"Look at it this way. Our little online magazine could use the boost this scoop would bring. Just imagine it, *CJ's Otherworldly Experiences* exposes a band of self-proclaimed warlocks on a mission to destroy the world with a book of black magic spells. It would probably shoot us to the top of the paranormal magazine heap. All it takes is one thoroughly researched, fact-based article to show we can compete with the best of them." She leaned toward Jenny. "We'll never have to work an odd job again to make ends meet. Sales will boom and who knows, maybe sponsors will place ads in our magazine as well."

"I hope you're right. I'd love to never wash a dish at the deli again. But I've got a nervous feeling this story doesn't have an ounce of *fact* behind it. That website you stumbled upon disappeared offline when you requested further information. For all we know, it was some computer geek kid playing around." Cait felt her questioning green-eyed stare even if she couldn't see it. "And you never did tell me where you got this so-called tip about this guy we're following."

Cait turned her gaze forward to the car slightly obscured by several other vehicles. "If you must know, I got it from him. I was at the pub last night. He was drunk and in need of a friend, so I sat beside him and listened to him slurring on about the mess he'd gotten himself into."

"You got it from a drunk. Now we've wasted a day following him." Jenny's voice cracked as she yelled at Cait. "I can't believe you. All that hooey about taking our magazine to the next level and you gambled it all on a bum's drunken tale."

"It's a believable tale. Why else was there a website recruiting members with any sort of magical powers?" she replied as confidently as she could. Thinking about it from Jenny's point of view spurred a bit of doubt on her judgment for a second but she refused to let it take root.

"The one that disappeared? The website we can no longer find online? You've dragged me all around town, following this idiot on a whim."

Cait grabbed Jenny's arm, not letting her escape the car. "It's not a whim. I know you've been paying attention. We've been discussing what he's been doing all day. We both know he's tailing that redhead. He let it slip she's the assignment he's been given. Even if it turns out not to be connected to something paranormal, aren't you the least bit curious as to why he's following this woman? What if he plans to hurt her?"

"Then shouldn't we tell the authorities, let them handle it? What are we going to do? Stop him?"

"If it looks like he's going to do her any harm," Cait looked around, "I'll run him over with the car."

Jenny burst out laughing. "He'll do more damage to this old thing than it'll do to him."

"Probably," Cait agreed with a laugh. Jenny wasn't too far off when it came to the

1963 Volkswagen Bug. But she loved it, duct-taped rear bumper, faded gray paint, rust spots and all. "At least we'll get his attention and give her time to escape if nothing else."

Jenny cleared her throat. "You know, we've researched a lot of strange, unexplainable things since we started this magazine, but we've never tailed anyone before. It's kind of got me a bit on edge."

"Me too," Cait admitted as she shifted in her seat to face Jenny better. "You've got to admit it's been fun. No. More than fun. It's a thrill and you know it. Kind of like when we discovered the truth about the college campus ghost and exposed it in the *Campus Tribune*. Remember?"

"How could I forget? That was the start of our paranormal sleuthing career." Jenny sighed. "Hard to believe it turned out to be a sleepwalking professor dressed as a woman."

"You and I were the only ones brave enough to get close enough to realize it was a man in drag. We did our research and found out the ghost showed up after a student died in a hit-and-run accident two years before we started school there. You discovered he was the professor who reported his car stolen two days after the accident. If we hadn't put two and two together and written a damn good article, he may've gotten away with it," Cait stated smugly.

"Guess he never realized how much a guilty conscience can fuck with one's psyche," Jenny replied. "You're right. Our article did make the police question him to the point he confessed and even gave up the location of the car he'd dumped in the lake."

"We went chasing a ghost and caught a murderer. It's what gave us the bug to start our magazine. We write articles about ghosts and paranormal activities and determine between fact and fiction. Granted, the professor was the only bad guy we've helped catch." Cait nodded toward their suspect. "What if he's up to something just as sinister? You and I might be the only ones to save the woman he's tailing. If we call in the authorities now, what proof do we have to give them that he's up to no good?"

"We've got nothing." Jenny's tone took on a determined edge. "How do we handle this? What if he really is a killer? Or worse, what if this brotherhood wants him to kidnap this woman as a sacrifice for some demonic ritual?"

"So now you're getting on board with the devil-worshiping brotherhood," Cait teased.

"I'm leaning that way. It'd make a much better headline. *Demonic Brotherhood Attempted Sacrifice of Woman.* Anything else is newspaper fodder."

Cait laughed. "Now that's the Jenny I know. Put a catchy header on it and sell, sell, sell."

"Damn right. Gotta keep our small-time mag going." Jenny burst out laughing right along with Cait. After a moment her laughter stopped suddenly as she said, "It just hit me, Cait. What was he doing in the bar if he was supposed to be following that woman? Shouldn't he have been watching her in case she moved instead of sitting on a stool beside you drinking?"

"I asked him that last night." Cait swallowed any remaining laughter. "He told me and I quote, 'The old bat's in bed for the night'. He needed a drink to cope with the loneliness. Can you believe he even hit on me, wanting me to hang out with him while he sat watch?"

"Really." Jenny nearly squealed as she spoke. "Bet he wanted to do the backseat bongo with you to pass the time. You could've fucked the info out of him, Cait, instead of having us traipse all over town today."

Cait pffted then said, "Like that was going to happen." Laughter broke out between the giddy pair again.

When a man in a wheelchair and a redheaded woman exited the restaurant, the pair's laughter quieted.

"Is that her?" Jenny asked. "I can't get a good look at her."

"Aye," Cait answered.

A sleek van was brought around. The driver got out. Cait noted he walked with a distinguishable limp as he moved around the van and lowered a lift gate from the side to accommodate the chair. The man rolled onto the lift and was placed into the van, and then the woman was escorted to the opposite side. She got into the passenger seat. Once they were settled, the driver took his position behind the wheel. The second it pulled into traffic, the man they were watching pulled out behind it. Cait followed suit. She couldn't help but pick on Jenny.

"Looks like the game's afoot, Watson."

Jenny jested in return, "Okay, Sherlock wannabe. Let's just hope Moriarty doesn't beat us again this time."

Though she loved Cait's enthusiasm, this adventure had her stomach in knots. They'd never done anything this *thrilling*, as Cait called it. The campus ghost story just happened to have a happy ending. This one might not. She wasn't cut out for that type of crime-related journalism. Catching murderers wasn't her thing. It was why they followed the paranormal route. Jenny adjusted her seat belt and settled in for the ride.

Discussing their first paranormal investigation had her thinking of how they met. She could still picture Cait as a young exchange student at The University of Texas at Austin who was assigned as Jenny's dorm roommate. Cait's voluptuous shape was a stark contrast to Jenny's long, lean frame. The feisty-spirited brunette with deep-brown eyes that always held a sparkle of laughter in them was the complete opposite of Jenny's mild-mannered frankness with a twist of let's-not-do-that-we-might-get-hurt attitude. If it wasn't for Cait's adventurous nature, she might still be a meek scaredy-cat, sitting in her room reading about paranormal adventures instead of living them.

Cait had changed her. Made her more outgoing. She snorted. With older brothers, you would've thought she'd be a tough tomboy, but no. Her mom wanted a girl and made sure she was a girly-girl. She'd never had to fight for anything ever. Her brothers protected her as if she were some sort of fragile flower. Jenny leaned her head against the seat rest as she kept her eyes on the taillights of the suspect's car. What would her overprotective brothers think of her now, chasing after a weirdo? They'd tell her not to do it, that's what.

She shot a sideways glance at Cait—a disorganized, outgoing mess paired with a detail-oriented, shy individual. Definitely not a perfect pairing for an everlasting friendship, but somehow they'd made it work. Thanks to their mutual curiosity about all things paranormal. The night Cait caught her reading a book on Bigfoot broke the strained existence between them.

As a child, she'd dreamt of being the first to find proof that Nessie truly existed. When Cait admitted she'd had that same dream, Scotland was the logical choice for them to start their new life after college. Having a native as a best friend made the transition easier for Jenny. Her move hadn't thrilled her family. That discussion replayed in her head on occasion. She shivered. Confrontation wasn't her strong suit, especially where her family was concerned. She was her mother's only daughter. Jenny's six siblings were boys. Her mother resisted any sort of change when it came to her angel, but finally accepted it when she realized how happy this job made her little girl. Jenny made a mental note to call home as soon as possible.

Eventually she knew she'd have to tell her mom that she and Cait had taken a small flat in London. That was a conversation she did her best to avoid. As long as her mom believed they were staying with Cait's grandmother outside Edinburgh, Scotland, they were considered safe. The moment she found out they were living in a big city… Jenny tried to convince herself she hadn't told her mother because she didn't want her to worry. In truth, she just didn't want to have to deal with the arguments about her safety her brothers would have started if they knew.

Not wanting to lose sight of the vehicle up ahead, Cait increased the car's speed, causing Jenny to lean into the seat. The acid in her stomach churned and her thoughts flipped back to the issue of the moment. What if he really did intend to harm the redhead? What the hell would they do about it?

What would her brothers do? They'd punch him, that's what. She wasn't a fighter. On reflex, she pulled her cell phone out and checked the signal bars. Three. Good. At least there was a possibility of calling for help as long as they didn't wander too far out of their provider's range. She rolled her eyes. Cell phones sucked sometimes.

Chapter Three

Her gut twisted into a knot and she could barely speak as a mixture of emotions sprang to life. Excitement, anxiety, fear and anticipation swirled into a potent concoction that made her insides churn. She'd seen the curse in action. She knew what to expect but with Jameson at her side, uncertainty tainted her steps. What if she was wrong? What if this pair of statues weren't who she thought they were? She'd look like a fool in front of him. After all, she'd only seen them in the background of a press picture in a newspaper. Never up close.

He handed her the key when they reached the door. Her fingers trembled as she inserted it in the lock while he pressed the code to deactivate the alarms. She cut a sideways glance at him. She'd asked him to believe the unbelievable and he'd agreed. What if she couldn't back it up? Would he change his opinion of her and call her a crazy coot like the ladies who were supposed to be her friends at the club?

When he looked at her and smiled, her fears vanished. Nope. He'd still believe in her even if she was wrong about these statues being the lost MacKinnon twins. She took a breath and turned the key. The lock clicked and she twisted the knob, pushing the door open wide enough for his wheelchair to pass. Once inside, she closed it behind them.

Jameson flicked a switch and the warehouse brightened with light. May blinked at the sudden change. The moment she regained focus, he waved his arm gallantly in front of him and pointed toward a wide pathway between two rows of large crates.

"The treasure you seek is at the far end near the loading dock."

May forced her uncertainties away. She smiled and prayed she was right about this. "You lead and I shall follow."

As he rolled down the pathway, he grabbed a crowbar from a tool cart and explained, "I had them re-crated for transport to the gallery. I planned to place them on display next month. If they are what you claim—" He shot her a drop-dead sexy grin across his shoulder that refortified her trust that her first thought was correct. The "sleeping twins", as he called them, were truly the cursed MacKinnon brothers.

"They are," she replied. "I just know it."

At the end of the row, he turned right and shoved the crowbar into the edge of an oversized crate. It was wider than it was tall, which accommodated the statues' reclined positions. May couldn't help but admire Jameson's upper body strength. It took him mere minutes to open the crate. She held the side until he rolled out of its way, then released it when he nodded. It landed with a bang, which made her jump even though she knew it would to happen.

May released a nervous laugh. Jameson popped a little wheelie, easing his chair onto the discarded wooden side and rolled forward to remove the packing material from around the statues. Her eyes widened and her mouth fell open. They were the most wondrous sight. Her heart leapt for joy as she simply stared at what she knew were the cursed bodies of Donnell and Dour MacKinnon. On autopilot, she helped until every shred of packing material was removed from around them.

Her hands shook as she gently caressed their faces. These two never knew what hit them. May shook her head. MacGillivray cursed them as they slept. They looked so peaceful, unaware over two centuries had passed. One lay on his side, an arm under his head for a pillow with the bottom leg straight, while the top leg was bent, supporting him from toppling forward. The other twin was on his back, an arm across his eyes, the other under his head. The arms they used as pillows and the tops of their heads touched.

Dressed only in kilts, Donnell and Dour were a perfectly matched set of young Scottish lairds if she'd ever seen them.

How they'd managed to be kept together after so much time and not been broken apart, she'd never know, but could only be thankful they were intact. She knelt as she held Jameson's gaze and took his hands in hers. Her smile broadened. "It's them. It's the MacKinnon twins. They're exactly how Akira described them."

"That's all I needed to hear." A menacing voice came from behind Jameson.

May sprang upright as Jameson spun his chair around to face the intruder, who stepped from behind a crate. The man stood at average height, wearing a long trench coat and a knit cap pulled low across his brow. Dressed all in black, he appeared pale. His scruffy five o'clock shadow added to his dirtiness instead of giving this particular man a bad-boy appeal.

May's stomach sank. It was the man from earlier. The man she'd noticed before she went into the art gallery to see Jameson. He *was* following her. What the hell could he possibly want with the statues? Then it struck her.

Brother Leod had to be behind this. Damn. She'd let her guard down and led them to the twins. May held on to Jameson's chair for support as she stood directly behind it.

"Who are you?" Jameson demanded.

"Not important. I'm here for the statues." With his hand in his coat pocket, he motioned as if he had a weapon. "Now move away from the crate so I can get a good look at my prize."

May noted Jameson's hesitation, his shoulders lifting emphasizing their broadness, but she wasn't about to let him get hurt by doing something stupid. She tightened her grip on his chair handles and leaned close to his ear.

"Let him think he's won for the moment," she whispered. He met her concerned gaze across his shoulder and gave her a slight nod. As if he'd conceded to the intruder, Jameson released his wheels and let May roll him to the side. May's thoughts whirled as she played out several scenarios in her head.

Was he really armed with a weapon in his coat pocket or was he just trying to intimidate them? He didn't look that strong. Maybe if she tackled him at the knees, he'd fall. Then if Jameson rolled onto his supposed gun hand, injuring it, she'd threaten him with the crowbar to remain still until the authorities arrived. From the side angle of his face, recognition sparked May's brain. She knew him. Or at least she thought she did. She stepped beside Jameson's chair. Her hands on her hips, she leaned a little to the right, studying his face.

When he realized she stared at him, he stopped taking pictures and sending them to someone with his phone. "What?" he shouted angrily.

"Just trying to get a good look at you," May tilted her chin as she spoke. "Don't want to miss any details for the police."

"Get back, you old bat," he screamed, wildly waving his coat pocket at her. This led May to believe she was right. He was faking it. He didn't have a weapon.

She took a step forward. He leaned back. His eyes widened. "I'll shoot you if you don't stop."

"I don't think you will," May replied calmly. She never took her eyes from his face, trying to keep his focus on her. "I doubt seriously you have a gun in your pocket or else you'd be pointing it in my face by now."

"You're pushing your luck," he sneered and tried to sound menacing. She heard the slight hitch in his tone, the lack of conviction in his threat.

With the intruder's attention on May, he wasn't watching Jameson, who carefully eased into a better position closer to the man. He quietly lifted the forgotten crowbar from its location in his chair beside him, keeping it out of the other man's view. May had an idea of what Jameson planned and moved again, causing the man to turn more, facing her, his back toward Jameson. It was all Jameson needed.

Thwack!

He swung the crowbar like a baseball bat and struck the man behind both knees, knocking his legs from under him. His forehead hit the upper edge of the crate containing the twins. May jumped back, getting out of the way of the falling man as he landed face first, unconscious on the floor. The cell phone he'd been urgently using went sailing into the crate, sliding to a stop out of sight behind the statues.

"Nice swing," May praised as she high-fived Jameson. "That ought to teach that thug not to mess with us."

Jameson grinned, then changed instantly to somber. "How'd he get in here past Charles?"

May shook her head. "No clue. I doubt he was capable of hurting him."

She knelt to check the man's pulse. He was alive but bleeding from the cut on his forehead. Jameson pulled out his cell phone and dialed. It was answered on the first ring. "Charles, are you okay?"

A muffled male voice could be heard but she couldn't make out the words. "We've had a bit of a scuffle with a would-be thief. Contact the authorities and there's a need for an ambulance. No, not for one of us, the thief needs it." Jameson disconnected the call and looked at her.

"Charles drove to the local petrol station for fuel. He's safe, calling for help and coming back. Shouldn't be but a few minutes." Jameson sighed. "This wouldn't have happened if I'd remembered to lock the door behind us."

"It's not your fault." May stood. "Is there a first-aid kit? I think we should put something on his head to stop the bleeding."

Jameson rolled backward. "I'll get it and some duct tape to bind his hands in case he wakes."

"That won't be necessary," a rather large man stated in a heavy British accent as he sauntered toward them with a gun in his hand. Three other men followed along behind him, each wearing similar black hooded jackets and gloves. They kept the hoods up and used bandanas to conceal their faces like the old Wild West bank robbers. Only their eyes were visible. To May, none of the oversized goons looked as if they had an ounce of niceness in their bones.

She tilted her chin and faced off with the leader. "He might bleed to death."

He shrugged. "No major loss. It's the statues we're after."

"You can't have them," May informed him while standing her ground between the statues and the large man, who glared at her from beneath his hood.

He directed the others without shifting his eyes off her. It was a mute order. His team was already in motion as if everything had been planned. "Open the cargo door, get the lift and hurry. I'm sure the cops are probably on their way thanks to the bleeding idiot."

May watched as they moved with precision and speed. She needed to do something before they succeeded in stealing the twins. The echo of the roll-up door could be heard and the sound of a motor running slipped in behind it. Yep, it was obvious they'd orchestrated this job well. A knot tightened her chest but she didn't back down. Keeping her cool, she asked, "How'd you get here so quickly? I'm assuming you were the one he sent the text messages to."

The man snorted, relaxing the hammer of the gun. "He's simply a small fish in a big pond. We've been casing this place ever since the boss saw a picture in the paper. Idiot was given you as an assignment to follow. It was his dumb bad luck your path crossed ours. We've been watching, waiting for the right moment." He nodded at the unconscious thief lying in a small puddle of blood. "Only good thing he's done is lead us to an open door and a disabled alarm."

Jameson couldn't believe he'd been that stupid. Should've locked the door and reset the alarm system. Idiot. Jameson grabbed May's arm. Her gaze met his. Anger mixed with fear was clearly visible in her eyes. He couldn't let her do something irrational. Jameson was certain May hadn't told him everything about the statues. Why would thieves want these particular statues? The warehouse was brimming with expensive and more easily portable artwork. It didn't make sense.

Did the intruders think the same thing about them as May? That they were cursed? The first thief claimed he was glad to hear May's declaration about them being

MacKinnons and he'd called them his prize. He'd been taking pictures and sent them to his associate, who was now here to collect the statues. Who was this boss who had May followed, and why? So many questions cluttered his brain. No matter what, he needed to keep May safe, and facing off with an armed robber wasn't exactly the thing she should be doing as far as he was concerned.

He slid his hand down her arm to capture her hand as he tried to defuse the situation before she got herself shot. Taking a deep breath, he turned his attention to the leader of this gang of thugs. "Why do you want these statues? I can pay you more than whoever you're working for to leave them and go away."

The ringleader laughed maniacally. "Typical rich asshole thinking money can buy everything. In this case, you lose."

Jameson had to think fast since the other three men had slid the tines of the lift under the crate and were manipulating it for transport. "Then tell me, what's more important to you than financial security?" he implored, hoping to stall for time in order to allow the police to arrive. He didn't like the fact May's grip tightened on his hand as they lifted the crate and the statues wobbled inside.

It was obvious they had no intentions of packing it properly.

"Might as well throw his ass on top and carry him out of here." The leader continued doling out orders.

Two of them lifted the unconscious man and tossed him on top of the wooden crate. Jameson felt May flinch when his head bounced as he landed hard. It was obvious they really didn't care about him. They were simply cleaning up the loose ends.

"You didn't answer my question," Jameson reminded the thief.

He pointed the gun at Jameson. "It's about power. Power the likes of which the world has never seen. And it's worth more than money."

"I demand to speak with Brother Leod," May insisted.

The man cocked his head sideways and said in a mocking tone, "Who?"

* * * * *

The moment the van pulled away, the man they followed slipped inside a warehouse behind the woman and the man in the wheelchair. Cait nodded to Jenny and together they exited the car, sneaked over to the warehouse and quietly entered the building. Slowly and deliberately, they got into a position where they could hear what was going on without being seen. For some reason, their suspect wanted some sort of statues.

What in the world did this supposed paranormal brotherhood want with a pair of statues? Cait needed to get a better view to determine what was so important about this particular item, when there were so many easier-to-steal artworks readily available. Carefully, she and Jenny worked their way into a better position. From their new angle, a pair of sleeping men, wearing kilts, was chiseled in stone.

The two lifeless forms had bodies even a Greek god would die for. Damn. Cait strained to get a look at the faces of the statues, but the man in the wheelchair blocked her line of sight. It impressed her how agile he was when he knocked the legs out from under their suspect, who hit his head and was out cold from what she could tell. Catching a motion out of the corner of her eye, she ducked behind the crate and huddled close to Jenny. Holding her finger to her lips and shaking her head, she let Jenny know not to say a word or move.

Heavy footsteps fell as Cait slowly peeked around the edge of the crate. A man carried a gun and was followed by three other men. All wore black and were there on a mission—to get those statues. They had to be extremely valuable. She kept a visual on them and listened to every word she could catch.

The thieves turned down money to go away. For what? Power? It didn't make sense. Had the guy they followed been right about the leader of the brotherhood wanting to become some *all-powerful* being, a black-magic guru? She'd scoffed at the idea when he'd said it. Now she was beginning to think he meant it.

She heard the woman demand to speak with a Brother Leod. She'd heard that name before in conjunction with the brotherhood they were investigating. Their suspect had let it slip while drunk at the bar. The way the oversized thug mocked the woman with his reply pissed off Cait. For some reason, she knew she couldn't let them steal these statues. If they made it past the crates where she and Jenny were hiding, then they'd be free and clear to load the statues into the waiting van without anyone stopping them.

That *so* wasn't going to happen.

The man with the gun took a step backward and before he turned, Cait acted on impulse. She rushed him, clipping him behind the knees and taking him face first to the ground. His heels dug into her stomach. Air gushed from her lungs, leaving her winded for a few seconds. She heard Jenny scream before she saw her fly off the top of a crate and land on two of the other thieves.

For a moment, Jenny couldn't believe Cait took a man down. She had no time to consider the consequences. Two of the other men were moving toward Cait and she'd have no part of them hurting her best friend. She'd watched enough WWF wrestling with her brothers to pick up a thing or two. All she could do was hope it worked. As nimble as a cat, she got on top of the crate she'd been hiding behind and pounced. With her arms and legs spread wide, she managed to hit the pair with enough force that one fell and the other stumbled backward.

She landed hard, half-on, half-off the man on the ground. Immediately he rolled, leaving her face first on the floor and out of breath. Though she gasped for air, she lifted onto her hands and knees. Funny, it didn't look like it hurt when those guys did it on TV.

The squeal of brakes had her twisting her neck to see what happened. The lift operator slammed the lift in park so hard the statues wobbled and the older woman held her hands out as if she could possibly have stopped them if they fell. From the size of them, she probably would've been crushed if they did topple over.

Before Jenny stood, one of the men kicked her in the ribs.

"Bitch," he spat out but didn't get the chance to connect again. At first, she had no clue what happened, since she'd doubled over in pain and her eyes automatically closed. Prying them open, she saw the guy who kicked her flat on his back, moaning, and the van's chauffeur limping quickly toward her.

A dark shadow behind her eyes threatened her consciousness. She had no intention of blacking out. Not when her best friend needed her. Jenny dug deep for the energy to stand and remain focused as the chauffeur helped her. She did plan to have a stern chat with Cait when this was over.

In her book, the definition of *thrilling* did not include jumping off a crate and getting the crap beat out of her. Nope. She wheezed taking in air though her side ached. This most definitely wasn't a thrill. She might've been raised in a house full of boys, but that didn't mean she knew how to fight. She never had to. Her brothers were always there to protect her. God, she wished she did know how right now though. The knee-to-the-groin trick her oldest brother taught her wasn't going to help in this situation.

She hated to admit neither she nor Cait had any fighting skills, but that didn't stop Cait. She caught sight of Cait holding her own, as was the chauffeur. He'd jumped into the brawl, slinging punches and bloodying a nose or two. Impressive for a driver. She didn't have time to think it through or ask questions. Jenny leaned against a crate, catching her breath and searching for a weapon. Seeing a loose board, she pulled it free and wielded it like a bat.

Blindly she swung it at anything wearing a black hooded sweatshirt. When she hit one of them in the side of the head, he slowly folded to his knees and fell over onto his side. It felt awesome to see it was the idiot who'd kicked her. She stood over him and sneered.

"Vengeance is mine," she quipped before turning on her heels and taking aim for anyone who came near her.

Cait quickly scooted onto her knees, even though it hurt to breathe. Definitely going to have a set of bruises on her tummy from the feel of it. She sat on his back, knees digging into his sides, and jerked his hood down, tightly wound her hands in his hair and tried to keep his face pressed to the floor. The way he was flailing about, attempting to dislodge her precarious position, had to be similar to riding a bull.

Wheelchair guy rolled into action, running over the man's hand before he retrieved the gun he'd dropped in the fall. The man screamed, barely drowning the sound of bones breaking. Cait cringed at the crunch and pop. Instead of weakening him, it incited his crazy gene even more. The large man rose straight onto his knees, cradled his injured hand to his chest and used his other hand to hit Cait, who clung to him like a backpack. With one hand twisted in his hair, she wrapped her other arm around his neck and squeezed, hoping to shut off his airway.

She was surprised to see the van's driver had appeared out of nowhere. He helped Jenny off the floor and then went to swinging punches at the other three. The man in the wheelchair spun, snatched up the crowbar and entered the mix. He landed a solid blow with the crowbar in the middle of one of the bad guy's guts.

As she battled to keep a hold on the ringleader, Cait caught sight of the older woman in front of the crate. Her head was bowed as if in prayer and the words of what Cait thought was an ancient Celtic prayer poured from her lips.

"Ceum saor de clach. Be Ye Biast air duine. Tis Gaol dara slighe. Ge Ye be mèinne dh'oidche mur dh'là."

The ground rumbled. The crate shook. Cracks splintered the statues. Light spilled from the newly formed slits as dust filled the air. Pebbles and stones rolled to the ground. A cloud of dirt and dust rose, filling the area to a point visibility was nil.

As if mesmerized by what was happening, the fighting momentarily stopped. Cait slid off the guy she'd been bronco riding. Coughing and gagging from everyone filled the room. When the dust cleared, Cait's jaw dropped. One word flashed inside her head. *Damn.*

A set of the most gorgeous twins she'd ever seen sat inside the crate. The statues were gone. Two living, breathing men were in their place. Granted they were covered in dust, but… Wow.

"You bitch," echoed around the warehouse as the forgotten injured man on top of the statue's crate sprang at the woman, knocking her to the ground and landing on her. His fist poised to hit her but never made contact.

A strong hand caught his wrist and held it tight, jerking him by his arm off the woman.

The wild-eyed man glared at the hand, then all color drained from his face once he made the connection as to who had a hold on him.

"Ye nay be hitting the lady. Bad enough ye knocked her down." The tall Scotsman with fiery-red hair and the greenest eyes Cait had ever seen on a man turned his head to look at the other Scotsman and said, "What say ye, Dour, shall we teach this gent some manners?"

"Aye, in due time, *mi brathair*," Dour replied as he helped the woman, who'd been knocked to the ground, back to her feet. Confusion furrowed his brow as he obviously surveyed his surroundings. "Do ye happen to know where we are perchance?"

"Donnell, Dour," the redhead said. Her voice shook with excitement as the twins' faces showed their disbelief that this woman knew their names. "You've been set free from a curse. You've been asleep for over two hundred years. There are constraints with this freedom."

Donnell released the man he was holding as he stared, bewildered, at her.

"This isn't happening," the large ringleader spouted angrily. "It's some sort of trick. They've got the statues. Get them." He commanded his goons to attack.

"There's no time to explain. These men are out to destroy your family," she explained hurriedly as she pointed at the men dressed in black. "Help us and we'll see to it you're returned home safely."

Chapter Four

All hell broke loose. The ringleader rushed one of the tall Scotsmen. The Scotsman, whom Cait mentally labeled hunk number one, turned and laid a shoulder into him. He shoved the bad guy backward into a stack of crates. Dazed but not down, the ringleader came right back at hunk one.

"Donnell, ye be needing a hand with that one?"

"Nay, there be plenty to go around," he replied as he got wrapped up in a one-armed bear hug meant to crush him from his opponent.

The injured man, who had knocked the red-haired woman down, didn't remain standing for long. Wheelchair guy grabbed a fist full of his shirt, jerked him forward and landed a hard left to the side of the man's head. He crumpled to his knees.

Hunk two, whom Cait overheard being called Dour, sprang into the brawl as if it were his job. A bad guy had Jenny pinned against a crate and was about to hit her, when his wrist was broken by Dour. Cait saw Jenny cringe at the sound. She'd done the same thing when the ringleader's hand was damaged by the wheelchair. It was a sound she hoped not to hear coming from her or Jenny during this throw down.

She and Jenny had seen their fair share of pub fights, none of which they'd participated in. Nothing topped this one. Wheelchair guy had the red-haired woman safely behind him while he held the crowbar at the ready. The man he knocked out lay in a heap on the floor.

The chauffer was slugging it out with one of the hooded men, exchanging punch for punch. Dour dispensed with the man, whose wrist he'd broken, and was bobbing and weaving in a match against the last of the three, the man Jenny had hit in the head with the board. Somehow he'd gotten back on his feet and seemed madder than ever. Jenny was cheering Dour on and punching the air. Cait would've laughed if she wasn't so busy trying not to be in the way of that crazed ringleader dude. Broken hand and all, he didn't back down. Donnell placed himself between her and the monster of a guy. It seemed pain added to his craziness.

A hard blow bloodied Donnell's nose. A cocky grin split his face and Cait got the sense he loved the fight. "Is that all ye got?" came out of his mouth and she knew she was right.

The ringleader lunged at Donnell, causing him to take several strides backward. Cait couldn't move fast enough and became stuck between Donnell's backside and a crate. Her nose meshed into the space between his shoulders, and for a second she thought it snapped from the intense pain that shot between her eyes and made them water. Absently she grabbed his waist for support.

"Hang on, lassie," he said. Those sharp green eyes gazed at her from across his shoulder. Mischief made them sparkle. "We've got to move."

She did as instructed and held on, following his lead. He turned. She turned. He stepped. She stepped. Not sure why, she never let go and moved in sync with his actions. He bobbed. She bobbed as if they were connected as the men swung blow for blow. Some made skin-to-skin connections. Other punches did not, but that didn't stop them. What neither realized was where they'd relocated wasn't the best of spots. Cait backed up, lost her footing and toppled backward into the van. It wasn't a far fall, just enough of a dip between the loading dock of the warehouse and the van for her to lose her balance and land on her bottom.

Donnell tried to catch her. The momentary lapse of eye contact with the ringleader was all the man needed. He blindsided Donnell with a sucker punch to the side of the head, then a hard shove from behind sent Donnell onto his hands and knees into the back of the van.

"If I can't have the statues," the ringleader sputtered, angrily and out of breath, "then I'll bring him you."

Before either moved, the door slammed shut and locked. Seconds later the van lunged forward. Cait crawled to the door and tried to lift the gate. It wouldn't give. She sat back on her heels.

How in the hell had she gotten herself into this?

Jenny shoved from behind Dour as he landed the final blow to his opponent. She ran toward the departing van, unable to believe what had happened. Without a word, she jumped to the ground and ran as fast as her long legs would carry her. It'd been years since she ran track in college, but she'd maintained a daily regimen of jogging. This she was thankful for as she rounded the corner on the tail of the van. A few seconds after it passed, she was at the Beetle's driver's side door and sliding into the seat. There was no way she was losing sight of that van. It carried her best friend as a hostage.

Dour slid to a halt in the open door of the car. That was the first she noticed he'd been right behind her. Gasping for air, she at him. "I don't have time to waste. Either you get in or you stay behind. I'm going after my friend."

"*Mi brathair* also has been swallowed by that monster. I am going. I no understand this beast ye be in. Where are the horses?" He looked around frantically.

"There are no horses," she shouted, leaned over and opened the passenger door. "Now get in."

He ran to the other side, hesitated for an instant, then slid onto the seat. She had the engine on and shifted into gear the moment his butt made contact with the cushion. With a stomp on the gas, the car lunged forward, causing his door to slam shut.

Jenny hated driving Cait's baby this way, but she had no choice. She gave her passenger a quick glance and knew something was wrong. He held on tight to the dashboard and his eyes were wide with fear.

She huffed. "I know I'm going a bit fast here, but my driving isn't that bad." If she didn't know better, she thought she smelled fear wafting off him.

His voice cracked as he spoke. "Milady, this be a first for me."

"You've never ridden in a car?" She couldn't hide the surprise in her voice. In this day and age, that was practically unheard of, everyone rode in or drove a car.

"There are no such things where I come from."

Then it hit her. In her panic to chase after her friend, she'd forgotten the magical miracle she'd witnessed at the warehouse. He was one of a set of twins who — if the older woman was to be believed — had been released from a two-hundred-year-old curse. She slanted her eyes his way for a second, taking in his dust-covered appearance. Pebbles littered his red hair, which was straight, loose and came to just below his shoulders. Jenny darted her eyes forward, determined not to lose sight of the van.

She'd felt the floor shake and heard the stone crack. For a few moments she'd been blinded by bright light spilling from the statues. She cleared her throat and still tasted the dust that had filled the air. Was it a miracle? Was he one of two who were cursed?

Did she believe in curses?

Jenny loosened the death grip she had on the steering wheel. She believed in everything paranormal. It was why she and Cait got along so well. They loved the supernatural, the hunt for the truth behind the tale. Their online magazine was proof of their conviction to the unusual and different. Look where that landed them. In a life-or-death situation, that's where. God knew if Cait was okay or not. She'd taken a pretty decent fall into the back of that van. Jenny chewed her lower lip.

Behind her in the distance she heard the faint sound of sirens. The authorities must have arrived at the warehouse. A tad too late in her opinion. She pulled her cell phone from her pocket and dialed for help. It seemed like forever before the emergency dispatcher answered. The moment the connection was made, Jenny spoke quickly, and gave every detail she could.

"I witnessed a kidnapping at a warehouse in the East India Dock region. Several criminals attempted to steal from the warehouse but were stopped by a fight that broke out. They kidnapped two people. A woman, brunette, average height and weight and a man." She paused and glanced at the identical version beside her. "Long red hair, tall and muscular in build." She wasn't about to tell them he was probably over two hundred years old. They'd think she was nuts. "My friend and I are tailing the perpetrators, who are in a black van. It took a left onto the highway and we're staying on—" She pulled the phone from her ear and grumbled, "Damn. No signal. Dropped the call.

"Just fucking wonderful," Jenny groused. That meant the one on Cait was probably useless as well. Frustrated, she tossed the cell phone into the backseat without taking her eyes off the van. She couldn't believe how busy the late-night traffic was in this area, but was grateful for the camouflage to help her pursue without being easily seen. If they saw her, they'd probably do everything in their power to lose her.

She should've listened to Cait and gone with a more reliable cell carrier rather than the cheapest. Being the frugal bookkeeper wasn't exactly helping them out in this moment of dire need, now was it? She rolled her eyes at her own stupidity.

Jenny stared straight, keeping the van in sight. The lives of two people were in her hands and she had no way to call for help. Her only assistance in this venture was a man who was deathly afraid of the car. Hopefully the police had been given as much information as possible at the warehouse and were now on the trail following them. She highly doubted it.

Deciding to try to make the situation go a little easier, Jenny started a conversation. "My name is Jenny Baker. What's your name?"

"My name be Dour MacKinnon." The deep timbre of his voice resonated in the compact car. She'd find it soothing if he wasn't so distraught and his words strained. In a different scenario, she would've found it funny a big, strong macho guy acted like such a baby.

"Okay, Dour." She tried to sound friendly but the situation didn't exactly bode well as a first date, get-to-know-you sort of thing. This was all about Cait, his brother and a van in the distance with a gun-toting madman in it. Something in her gut told her she'd need his help if she wanted to succeed when they reached wherever it was they were going. "I'm not sure I believe this curse thing. But I know what I saw. So answer me this, how'd you survive if you were locked in stone for hundreds of years? How come you didn't age?"

The tall man seemed to relax just a smidgeon as he leaned into the seat, but didn't let go of the dashboard. His fingers tightened when she took a curve a bit too fast. She almost laughed but swallowed it instead as she waited for him to answer.

"Milady, I know not how this happened nor how *mi brathair* and I survived. What the woman spoke..." He paused then continued. She felt his gaze on her and she met his eyes for a moment. "Do ye know if it be truth or a lie?"

She truly didn't know. If it weren't for her headstrong friend, she'd be on the couch watching a made-for-TV movie and eating popcorn right about now. Instead, she was giving a wild pursuit through the outskirts of London to God knew where with a confused, albeit extremely handsome, man as her copilot.

"Let's go with it being the truth." Jenny forged ahead, turning her eyes back to the van's taillights in the distance. She was doing her best to keep a satisfactory space between them and the van without losing it. Granted this was Cait's forte, not hers. Jenny rarely drove during their escapades. "Any idea how you were cursed or who did it?"

His head shook as he answered, "Nay. Last I remember was getting knee deep in my cups with *mi brathair*, then going to bed. Next thing my eyes see be ye standing between two men."

"I was the first thing you saw?" She couldn't believe it. Was he hitting on her at a time like this?

"Aye." His mouth opened as if to say something else, then closed without the words escaping.

"Where did you live?" she managed to ask, not sure if she wanted to keep talking to him or not. Part of her was flattered by what he said. Part of her was a bit put off by it.

"Castle MacKinnon outside of Lochsbury." He stared into the night. "Tell me, are we still in Scotland?"

"No. We're near London. Not exactly sure where we're headed at the moment."

"Which direction be London?"

She pointed. "That way."

He leaned forward, staring at the stars for several long seconds. Then in a matter-of-fact way stated, "We are headed toward Scotland."

* * * * *

May hugged herself as she paced. The police arrived within minutes of the van's departure. They had mere moments to discuss with Jameson's bodyguard and chauffer, Charles, about what had happened. Since he'd seen the transformation, they secured his silence about the event. As far as the police were to be told, a valuable statue had been destroyed during a scuffle with a band of thieves. From the amount of dust, dirt and rock debris in and around the crate, it was plausible.

As soon as Jameson and Charles explained the basics of what happened, an APB was put out on the van. Charles followed his boss' lead as he gave details to the officer in charge. It was evident he felt the incident was his fault because he'd left them alone at the warehouse to get gas. From his actions and tone of voice, May knew his loyalty to Jameson was sincere. Apparently, he'd been with Jameson since a couple of months after the accident that left him wheelchair-bound.

For a few moments, she stopped and watched from the window in the warehouse office. Two of the three hooded thugs were arrested. The other one must've escaped or made it into the van without being seen, because he was nowhere to be found in or around the scene. The man she initially thought she recognized, the one who entered the warehouse first and threatened them, was being loaded onto a gurney. Apparently, he was still unconscious, so an ambulance had been called to escort him to a hospital.

She wrung her hands as she turned and made another pass around the office. How the hell had she been so stupid? She'd set the twins free only to land them in immediate jeopardy. One was hostage in the back of a van. The other was chasing them through the countryside in a beat-up Volkswagen Beetle, according to Charles, who had made it around the corner in time to see him get in and the car speed away.

How was she going to explain this to the other MacKinnon brothers already freed from the curse? Oh God, she had to tell them. Maybe they could help. May walked outside to Jameson's van and retrieved her cell phone from her purse. This was going to be a hard call to make. She leaned against the van for support. Her legs were so tired, as was the rest of her, but she had to do this, she had to make this call.

Ericka answered on the second ring. May took a breath. "Ericka, I'm sorry to be calling so late."

"It's okay, Aunt May. I'm hoping it's good news at this hour." Ericka sounded groggy from being awakened.

"I found the twins, but—"

"Really!" Ericka squealed. "So they were the pair of statues you saw in the paper?"

May could see the image of Ericka in her head clearly. She'd be dressed in one of her husband's shirts, her auburn hair a tangled bed-head mess and a hunk of a man wrapped around her snuggled beneath the covers. By now, Gavin would be sitting upright at her side in bed. His arm was probably around his pregnant wife and he was more than likely leaning with his ear close to the phone to hear the conversation.

"Yes, I was right. But…" May huffed heavily into the phone. "I'm afraid I've got some bad news."

After a second of silence, Gavin's voice came through the phone. "May, what be the trouble? Need me and *mi brathairs* in London?"

"Aye, Gavin," May admitted sadly. "A situation has arisen and I truly believe Leod is behind it. I've spoken the anti-curse. Your brothers are free to suffer the partial release. I didn't get the chance to explain it to them before I lost them."

She started to cry. Gavin's usually soothing deep brogue did nothing to ease her distress though she knew he tried. "May, suffer no pain because of your effort to help. It be because of your love that any of us are free."

May did her best to hold back her tears while she tried to tell Gavin what happened. "One of the twins is a hostage in the back of a van. I have no clue where they were headed. The other is in a car in pursuit of the van."

"*Och*, what a way to learn about the horseless carriage," he joked and she knew he tried to cheer her. He cleared his throat. "*Mi brathairs* and I are on our way. Ye can fill us in on the details when we arrive at your hotel."

"Thank you, Gavin."

"You okay?" Jameson asked from behind her. She'd been so focused on trying to speak with Gavin she hadn't heard him arrive. May disconnected the call, wiped her eyes and turned to face him.

"Not really," she said, forcing a thin smile. "I made a horrible mistake. In my rush to find the twins, I let my guard down and Leod got the upper hand."

His right eyebrow rose. "I think there's a lot more to this story than you've shared with me so far." He took her hand and pulled her onto his lap. "Right now you're exhausted. I can see it in your face. The police are almost done here. When they are, Charles will drive us to your hotel."

She leaned against him, accepting the safe haven his lap offered. What a mess she'd made of things. "Thank you, Jameson. I don't know what I would've done without your help tonight." She brushed a kiss to his cheek. "You gave me the best present I could ever have asked of you."

His brows arched as he met her gaze. "As I remember it, we seem to have temporarily lost the gift. One's been taken from us and the other has run off in hot pursuit."

She smiled. "Temporarily. I like that term."

"I meant it, May. We will get them back."

Chapter Five

Cait sat down hard in the far corner of the van. She hugged her knees to her chest and lowered her forehead onto them. What a night. Here she was captive in the back of a van with no clue what the hell was going on other than the fact some lunatic brotherhood might be behind it. Ugh. Why did she listen to a drunken nutcase in a bar? Jenny was right. Jenny! She jerked the cell phone from her pocket. *No signal.* She couldn't call her or the authorities.

Ohmygod. She prayed Jenny was okay. If they survived this, Jenny would never let her forget this ordeal. A crazy man and his hooded band of misfits, a guy in a wheelchair and a lady, all fighting over a crate of supposedly cursed statues. It sounded like a really bad B-movie.

She searched her thoughts, hoping to piece together what might've happened to Jenny. Everything occurred so fast. Squeezing her eyes tight, Jenny came into view in her mind's eye. The last she'd seen Jenny, one of the hunky twins was defending her.

The other twin ended up in here with her.

She lifted her head and opened her eyes but it was too dark to see. She pulled a soft leather manicure case from her back pocket. She'd converted it into a practical emergency supply kit. Jenny picked on her for carrying it everywhere, but she didn't care. Now she was grateful she had it. Cait slid the zipper open and felt for the miniature flashlight. Once she located it, she pushed the button. The light wasn't bright, but it was enough to see whatever she pointed it directly on.

Quickly, she evaluated the contents of the kit—a small multi-tool pocketknife, a full book of matches, bandages, a foil packet of antibiotic cream, a couple of alcohol wipes, a tiny bottle of hand sanitizer, a spare battery for the flashlight, tweezers, a nail file, a needle, a thin packet of thread and a firecracker just because you never knew when you were going to need one. Her eccentric uncle's words whispered through her head and she smiled. Now there was a man who loved to blow up things. She zipped it closed, then panned the light around the van.

Her companion was crouched in the center as if ready to pounce. Holding the flashlight with her mouth, she scooted on her hands and knees over to him. Once at his side, she took the flashlight in one hand and touched his arm with her other hand.

"You okay?" Pure fear danced across his pale face and his skin was clammy.

"What sort of beast be this?" he demanded in a shaky voice.

Cait opened her mouth, ready to mock his choice of words but her voice stalled in her throat. Had what she'd seen at the warehouse been real? Was it a magic trick of sorts or were they really two men cursed as the older woman claimed? She'd heard the woman speak a beautiful verse and saw the statues shake and crack. Dust filled the air so thick nothing could be seen. When it settled, two gorgeous men sat in the statues' place. Had they somehow replaced the statues with living, breathing men while visibility was nil? Was there a trapdoor under the crate like that of a magic show's stage? So many questions cluttered her brain to the point her head hurt.

Deciding to play along until she figured it out, she simply answered his childlike question. "This is a cargo van."

"What be a cargo van?" He stumbled over the words as if they grated his tongue.

Cait rolled her eyes. So this was how he planned to play it. "A cargo van is a motorized vehicle, which is larger than a car and used to haul big loads."

"Milady, I no understand. Where are the horses?"

She licked her lips as she configured her response. Now really wasn't the time to play twenty stupid questions. "Listen, I'm not sure if I believe in this curse bit. So if'n you're an actor playing a part, you might want to stop now. Whether you realize it or not, we've been taken hostage and are locked in here for lord knows how long by lord knows who."

His stare hardened as if he'd considered her words and found them offensive. "Lassie, I know not of which ye speak. I am no actor. I am a hostage same as ye. My name be Donnell MacKinnon of Clan MacKinnon. Last I remember I was lying in a drunken stupor next to *mi brathair*. How I came to awaken in this foreign location be a puzzle."

Even though she wasn't totally buying the cursed-man thing, she did believe he was in the same boat. They both were locked in the back of this van against their will. She sat back on her heels and kept the light where she could see his face without it being directly in those gorgeous green eyes.

Casually, she let the light flicker over the rest of him. In the warehouse, she'd gotten a decent look at him that had sparked her libido. Now he was all hers to enjoy. A bit of dirt and dust coated his flesh, adding validity to the cursed theory. Okay. So *if* he was a man who'd been imprisoned in stone, he had to be in need of a good woman. What better way to kill time while waiting to find out where they were going and why? Maybe, just maybe, he'd let slip *who* he really was and what was going on *if* his guard was down.

And when was a man's guard down?

She smiled, remembering the advice of her Gran. *If'n you ever want to know the truth from a man, ask him during sex. The blood seeps from the brain to his dick, lowering his mental locks and loosening his lips. If'n that don't work, get him drunk.* She almost laughed out loud at the memory. Now there was a woman with spirit. Cait looked at Donnell and knew what Gran would do if'n she were a younger lass. She'd go for it. A grin split her lips. This was one piece of advice she didn't mind taking.

Since she didn't happen to have any liquor handy, sex seemed to be the justifiable method of choice. If she played him just right, he'd drop this act and his real identity would surface. If nothing else, she'd at least have a good time while being bounced around like a couple of balls. Might as well bounce for fun.

Sex was sex, plain and simple, and with a hunk like this one, all she hoped was that he wasn't gay. It'd be just her luck. Locked in a van with a gorgeous man and she wasn't his flavor. She slid a little closer and tested the waters. Being confined with him was making her horny. Or was it the fear of possibly dying at the end of this trip making her hormones run rampant with the idea this might be her last chance at a good tumble? She shrugged. It didn't matter which. She needed information and was willing to make the sexual sacrifice to get it.

Cait positioned the light so she could see his face and he could see hers. "MacKinnon, if what you say is true, it's been a really long time for you and I know it's been quite a while for me." She stretched upward and leaned closer, giving him her best wickedly inviting smile. "What say you to a bit of sex? If'n I'm going to die when this van stops, at least I'll go out happy."

Boldly she slid her hand under his kilt and up his thigh. His eyes widened with surprise that quickly flashed into desire the moment her fingertips made contact. *Nice* was the only word that filled her thoughts at the flesh in her hand.

"Milady, no let it be said a MacKinnon denied a lady's request. Would nay be gentlemanly."

Sheer heat scorched her from her lips to her toes when his mouth took command of hers. The man could kiss. She had to give him that one. His hands skimmed her arms then cupped her arse, causing her to shiver. Before she lost the flashlight, she managed to tuck it in the front pocket of her jeans. The head of the light pointed out of her pocket, illuminating the area as best as possible.

As she caressed him, he twitched and hardened. Oh baby, she needed to be naked and fast. Cait released him and separated from the kiss. As she untucked the shirt from her jeans, he grabbed the material and pulled it up her torso. Apparently, he wanted her naked as well. Cait crossed her arms and lifted it over her head and dropped it at her side. His hands found her breasts as his face nuzzled between them.

"I do love a well-endowed lass," he claimed. The heat of his breath to her skin sent chills across her breasts and straight to her nipples, instantly turning them to steel points. As if he couldn't wait for her to remove the bra, he lifted her breasts from the cups, thumbing her areolas in gentle circles before flicking each nipple once with the tip of his tongue.

Moisture flooded her panties. Damn. He was good at getting her wet with his skilled foreplay. She second-guessed the rapid response of her body. It had to be the stress of the situation heightening the effects of his ministrations. All thought left her brain when his mouth engulfed a breast, sucking it in deep, grazing its tender flesh with his teeth, then capturing the nipple in a pleasurable tug. If she wasn't wet before, she definitely was now.

Cait squirmed, wanting to ride him hard and fast. She popped the hooks on her bra and flicked it off her arms. She undid her jeans and attempted to graciously wiggle out of them as she toed off her flats. Hot, naughty sex was the best. Doing it in the back of a van while being held hostage was a first, and the thrill of it had her hungry for this hunk. Danger excited her. Always had. As she fought with her jeans, he slid his hands along her bared flesh, making her wish she undressed faster. With the jeans off, she quickly laid them so the light was kept on them. She liked being able to see the gorgeous man.

His fingers found her slit and his mouth left her breast. Awe filled his tone. "My little minx be shaven clean. Ye are a treasure chest of surprises." Before she could think, he had her on her back and he lay between her thighs. "*Och.* To have the chance to taste ye *brèagha neamhnaid*—pretty pearl—without the nuisance of hair."

His tongue dug between the folds of her slit and nearly sent her over the edge with one skillful swipe. Any questions she wanted to ask about his identity dissipated into a purple haze as lust took full control. Cait lifted her hips, gyrating against his face. He cupped her buttocks while he feasted, licking and sucking her juices, pumping his tongue in and out of her, bringing her closer to orgasm. When he latched on to her clit and sucked it hard, she knotted her fingers in his hair and screamed as she peaked.

Her heart pounded as she gulped for air. He lowered her bottom and traversed her body, kissing and nipping a path along her skin. His face hovered above hers as he positioned himself between her thighs. Cait was already in heaven when he entered her. This was simply an additional layer of pleasure upon pleasure. Being at her partner's mercy wasn't normally her style but for now, it was rocking her world letting him do most of the work.

Swift strokes in and out caressed her inner muscles, sending phenomenal sensations to every ounce of her being. He kissed her long and sensually while balancing his weight on his legs and elbows, and still managed to thrust a steady rhythm. She relaxed, enjoying the thrill created by such a wonderfully skilled man. He wasn't her first, but he was the first to have caused such an explosive orgasm with what seemed to be minimal effort on his part.

As the crest rose again inside her, Cait gathered his face in her hands. She intensified their kiss, warring tongue against tongue in a valiant attempt to match his kissing ability. She needed harder. She planted her feet and pumped in time with his thrusts. Deeper. She liked this better. She'd taken a breather but now she was pushing him to increase their pace. She broke from the kiss and nipped his earlobe.

"It's my turn to lead this dance." Not sure how she accomplished it, she rolled them onto his back so she could ride him, wild, hard and fast. She knew she should be using the sexual distraction to do something other than enjoy, but for the life of her, she couldn't remember what she wanted to ask. Feeling him beneath her sent her thoughts into hyperdrive, focused strictly on their pleasure.

Donnell wasn't sure how he'd gotten where he was, but at the moment he wasn't complaining. His hands were full of a voluptuous woman who apparently liked to be on top. With his kilt balled around his waist, the lass had full access to his shaft, which was nicely situated inside her. He liked the bounce of her full bosom as she controlled their pleasure. The smooth flesh of her bottom teased his hands as he massaged the wondrous globes, urging her to rock back and forth in a generous motion.

He didn't have to guide this woman. She knew what she wanted and took it from him. *Och*, where had he landed? Were all the women here this adventurous? Releasing her buttocks, he caught her breasts in both hands, stilling their magnificently mesmerizing dance as she rode him. He hoped he read her wild-eyed gaze correctly and took a chance, pinching her nipples hard. Her head lolled back as she squealed in delight and moisture soaked him. A smile tugged at his lips. He'd guessed right. She liked it a bit on the rougher side of naughty.

Digging in his heels, he drove into her. She leaned forward, palms flat on his abdomen, and met him pump for pump. The second she nipped his nipple he nearly exploded. Pain mixed with pleasure spurred him onward. The beautiful wench knew how to give as much as she took. If she wanted a wicked ride, then he intended to give it to her.

He smacked her arse. Her eyes widened. Pure heat filled her dazed stare but she didn't miss a beat as she swiveled her hips round and round. The move made his bawls tighten. He was close. She leaned back while continuing to rock hard and heavy. He supported her by grabbing her luscious bottom. When she reached behind her and ran her fingernail along the sweet spot between his anus and bawls, he came undone. That move was unexpected and definitely one he liked.

Liquid heat spurted from him, as he remained cocooned within her sheath. She fit him perfectly. He liked the sensations of her inner muscles coaxing his shaft for every last drop as their pleasures combined. He knew he'd released her essence at least three times during this coupling, but was it enough for this magnificent woman? If not, she'd have to wait a bit for him to recuperate and then he'd more than happily try again.

He sighed heavily when she collapsed against his chest. Wrapping his arms around her, he was grateful for a moment to rest as he closed his eyes. Several long seconds passed before his eyes opened and he realized even a great bout of sex didn't change anything. They were still prisoners, locked in this moving beast she'd called a van without a clue as to where they were going or why they'd been taken.

Donnell prayed his *brathair* Dour was safe. The van hit a bump, bouncing them around. He tightened his grip and refused to lose hold of the woman.

"Ye are safe, lass," he reassured her when she tried to slide off him. He ran his fingers through her hair and kissed her brow as she settled back into place on top of him. Sadly, his shaft softened and lost its haven in her heat. Holding her gave him comfort and for some reason he spoke the words of his thoughts. "Do ye know what became of my family?"

"No," she replied softly. The warmth of her mouth caressed his chest as she spoke. "Until today, I didn't know you existed." Her head shifted and she stared at him. "You truly believe you are a MacKinnon cursed for over two hundred years?"

"Aye."

"I promise you, if'n we make it out of here alive, I'll help you find them." The sincerity in her voice touched him.

He caressed her cheek. "I make ye a promise, lass. We shall survive this."

His words seemed to soothe her because she relaxed in his arms. The sound of a low snore floated to his ears and it made him smile. She'd fallen asleep. At least it didn't match the wall-rattling sound his twin made when passed out drunk. Donnell didn't move, wanting her to rest. He sensed there'd be no chance for such when they reached their destination. Keeping one arm around her, he used his other as a pillow for his head. With his eyes closed, images of a past long gone filtered through his thoughts.

Had any of his other *brathairs* been freed? The redhead hadn't said. Yet again, she'd not been given a chance considering the circumstances. He and Dour woke in the middle of a struggle, which had apparently been about them. But why? It made no sense.

His family, his *brathairs*, were felled by a curse. Those words had to have been spoken by someone with a strong hate against his clan. It took no more than a second before the possible culprit surfaced in his memories. One face burned bright and his eyes sprang open. MacGillivray. The coward of a man had to be the arse to have done such a thing. Tavia wasn't his to claim. She'd wed his *brathair*, Gavin. That should've ended it. Donnell bet it didn't. Every fiber of his being wanted to strike out against this man, to cause him harm he'd never forget.

She must've felt him tense as she shifted and mumbled something so softly he missed it. Donnell stroked her back until she was comfortable. Once the whisper of her snore fell into its melodic rhythm, his thoughts returned to his family.

The redhead knew of the curse and of his clan. She'd have the answers he sought. When he and Cait escaped, she'd be the second person he found. Dour would be the first. Donnell did his best to relax but his mind refused. He silently calculated possible plans of escape, none of which he knew would work since he didn't understand this thing in which they were held captive. Frustration ruled his thoughts.

The little he'd seen of this new world so far seemed fueled by magic. Strange light dotted the ceiling of the building they had been in. The people dressed in unusual clothing. Their attackers wore black hoods. The van—as she had called it—rumbled beneath him, making him wonder if it was hungry and if so would its driver stop. That would give him the opportunity he needed to fight for their freedom.

Donnell lay in wait, listening and hoping he'd be able to keep his word to the lass. They would survive.

Chapter Six

Jameson escorted May to her hotel room. Belvedere was excited to see her. He lunged off the couch where he snuggled with the sitter, Iris. May was so happy to have found her. She was the hotel owner's daughter. May liked that the family lived in a suite on the main floor and worked together to run the business.

Belvedere jumped up and down, barking until May squatted and gave him a comforting hug.

"Hello, Belvedere. I missed you," she said as he licked her face. His nubby tail wagged a mile a minute.

"Ms. May," Iris interrupted as she rubbed sleep from her brown eyes and pushed away a strand of dirty-blond hair that had escaped her ponytail. "Belvedere is an awesome friend. We went for a walk around ten p.m. as you suggested. Would you like me to walk him again before I leave?"

"No thank you, Iris. It's late," May replied as she stood to face the teenager. "He'll be fine until the morning." She dug in her purse for money to pay Iris but Jameson beat her to it.

"Here, young lady, it's obvious Belvedere had a great time." Jameson handed her a couple of hundred-pound notes. The teenager's eyes widened.

"That's way too much," she proclaimed, trying to hand it back. He covered her hand with his.

"Keep it. You earned it. Look how happy he is." He nodded at Belvedere, who seemed to know it was his cue to wag his tail and appear to be smiling with his tongue hanging out of the side of his mouth. "Besides, we were much later returning than anticipated."

She turned to May, holding the money out to her. "Ms. May?"

"Keep it." May smiled. "You really did make a friend in Belvedere. Would you be willing to help me with his walks for the rest of my visit here in London?"

Iris bounced excitedly, then lowered to her knees to rub Belvedere behind his ears. "Yes, Ms. May. I'd love to help with him."

"Great. Are you available to walk him in the morning?"

"Of course," she said as she stood and followed May to the door. "What time?"

"Whenever you get up and moving will be fine." May opened the door to find Charles parked outside in a chair. She raised an eyebrow but he simply nodded as if that were all the answer she needed.

"I'll escort the young lady to her family's suite and return momentarily." When he reached the elevator he looked back at her and sternly commanded, "Close the door and lock it."

Automatically, May did as instructed. She turned to face Jameson. "Is there a reason Charles was sitting outside my door?"

Jameson shrugged. "He's nutty that way when it comes to protecting me. I think he's feeling a bit guilty for what happened at the warehouse. He's pissed at himself for not making sure the door was locked before he left. Seeing as I plan to stay here tonight with you, he intends to guard that door."

May feigned annoyance. "I don't recall asking you to stay. That's mighty bold on your part."

He reached for her hand and tugged her toward him. "You and I have been friends a long time and I can tell you're on edge and worried. There's no way I'm leaving you alone tonight. I'll sleep on the couch." He pulled her into his lap. "I want you to rest, knowing I'll keep you safe and I'd never let anyone hurt you."

May wrapped her arms around his neck and kissed him. Ending the kiss, she pressed her forehead to his and said, "I'm so tired. I can't promise anything."

"Not asking for anything, just here to protect."

Jameson wheeled them into the bedroom. May slowly stood and excused herself to the bathroom. Leaning against the closed door, she stared at the mirror above the sink. One exhausted human stared back at her. Her night had started off strong, having dinner with Jameson. It only got better when the statues turned out to be the lost MacKinnon twins. Seeing them freed gave her momentary joy until the evening took a turn for the worse and both brothers disappeared into the night.

May moved to the sink, washed her face and brushed her teeth. She changed into her favorite sleeping attire, a soft cotton t-shirt-type nightgown covered in puppy pictures and paw prints. She didn't bother with a fresh pair of panties. Going commando at night was the healthier option in her opinion. After removing what was left of the pins in her hair, she ran a brush through it.

Exiting the bathroom, she wobbled as she leaned and tucked Belvedere into his doggie bed. At home he slept with her. Most hotels respectfully requested no animals in the beds, so whenever they traveled this bed came with them. Belvedere didn't seem to mind and somehow understood the rules when they weren't home.

Looking at the big empty bed, she decided she wasn't ready to lie down, not without checking on Jameson. Part of her wanted to bring him to bed and show him how much she wanted him. The other part of her wasn't sure they were at that point in their relationship. Not yet. When she entered the sitting room, Jameson was in a quiet discussion with Charles. She couldn't hear what they spoke about and by the time she got closer, Charles took the laptop, nodded to her and retreated to his post in the hallway. Jameson had made himself comfortable on the couch. His shoes and socks were off and his feet were up on the coffee table. He looked as if he belonged.

She couldn't help but smile.

"I'm sorry, were we too loud?" he questioned. "We tried to keep our voices low so as not to disturb you."

"No," she answered. "I'm too wound up to sleep. Do you think the police will find them?"

He patted the cushion beside him. "Come sit. I hope you don't mind, but I chose not to leave it in the hands of the authorities to find them."

She pursed her brows. "Care to explain?"

"Let's just say I've made many friends with special talents, Charles included. He's a former Navy SEAL with great location skills. It's just a matter of time before we've got something tangible to go on."

"Do you think he can find them? We have no clue where Brother Leod is holed up or where he's directed the twins to be taken."

"I believe with the technology we have access to," he nodded as he spoke in an encouraging tone, "we will find them."

She wanted to believe him. The determined look on his face eased the angst in her chest a smidgeon. She knew how devious Leod could be when it came to the destruction of the MacKinnon clan.

"How about a glass of wine?" she asked as she walked over to the minibar. She wasn't sure what to think at the moment. She'd been so close to bringing Donnell and Dour home only to lose them. Confusion and disappointment warred with exhaustion. "I could use one right about now."

"It's not polite to let a lady drink alone." He grinned.

May poured two glasses of merlot, then moved to the couch. He laid an arm along the back, motioning her closer. Having his shoulder as a place of rest was too inviting to ignore. Once she was settled, she lifted her glass and touched it to his.

"Here's to renewing old friendships once we've found the boys."

"We will find them, May," Jameson's said, his tone filled with confidence.

"I truly hope so." She took a sip, then leaned her head on his shoulder and snuggled closer.

He sensed the worry wafting off her as he brushed a kiss to the top of her head. Questions cluttered his thoughts. There was so much she hadn't told him about those statues. Never in a million years would he have believed curses were real, until she'd proven it to him tonight. At dinner, she'd asked him to believe in the unbelievable. He'd taken a chance and trusted her even though doubt had lingered in the back of his brain. She was beautiful, talented and insightful. The women at the country club were wrong. May wasn't crazy. Just outright smart and wonderful to the fault of loving and living her life to the fullest no matter what the cost.

Now that he had her back in his life, he planned to be a part of her future. In order for that to work, he needed to know the facts. Jameson asked softly, "May, will you tell me everything that's going on with the statues, the curse and the MacKinnon Clan? Who is this Leod?"

May repositioned, shifting more upright, and turned to look at him. Her chest rose and fell as she took a deep breath. He could tell she hesitated, as if deciding if he should know the answers. Her expression darkened as she started explaining and he got the sense the person she spoke of was hated. "Brother Leod, as he calls himself, is a direct descendent of the man who placed the curse on the MacKinnon brothers in the first place. He believes in a sort of rite of passage from the *Book of Shadows*."

"*Book of Shadows*?" Jameson stroked her hair, trying to soothe her angst.

"Leod's ancestor, Hume MacGillivray, felt jilted by a woman named Tavia, who married the eldest MacKinnon, Gavin. According to Gavin, Tavia never had any feelings for MacGillivray. But he didn't see it that way. He disappeared deep into the mountains and joined an obscure monastery. Instead of seeking solace, he plotted revenge."

May took another visibly deep breath and held Jameson's gaze. He read the sincerity in her eyes as she continued. "The monks were the keepers of a dark secret, which he discovered. They were the caretakers of a book of black magic, the *Book of Shadows*. It was their job to safeguard it from the likes of MacGillivray. But he found it and stole it."

"I'm guessing the curse he used on the MacKinnons came from that book," Jameson said.

She nodded. "From documents we found in the monastery's archives, he forced them to pledge their allegiance to him, thus calling his order, The Brotherhood of the Sons of the Servant of Judgment. The monks felt MacGillivray slipped into insanity out of fear of the darkness that lived within the book. Apparently, he became obsessed with the book's power and tested several of the spells. We found a notation about some sort of experiment he was performing from the book that went terribly wrong, but the monk's documentations aren't clear as to exactly what. Something scared him so badly he hid the book. Not long afterward, he fell down a steep stairwell and broke his neck. The monks believed the book reached out from its hiding place and killed him."

"That's a pretty powerful book. Why does Leod feel he's entitled to it?" Jameson questioned. The book didn't belong to anyone. If it contained black magic incantations meant for evil use, then it needed to be left hidden or found and destroyed so no other nutcase like Leod could chase after it again.

"MacGillivray created a prophecy after he hid the book. It basically stated one day a descendent of his would be born with magical talents, who would rid the world of Clan MacKinnon. Once that person found and destroyed the statues, the book would reveal its hiding place to him and the power would be his for all eternity."

"How did he have any descendents? Didn't he die soon after hiding the book?"

"He took steps to make sure a descendent would be born. He hired several men to bring three young maidens to him. He married each in a self-administered service and forcibly had sex with them until they were pregnant. His actions went against everything the monks represented. I wouldn't doubt if one of the monks helped him down the stairs." She shrugged. "After MacGillivray's death, the monks planned to deliver his wives to the closest church. The night before they were to leave, the few men loyal to MacGillivray disappeared, taking the women with them. As far as the monks were concerned, the women were in God's hands."

"Talk about vengeance from the grave," Jameson quipped, giving May a smile.

"Damn, I hadn't thought about it that way." She laughed as she shook her head. "Leave it to you to point that out."

"That's what I'm here for," he jested. "Comic relief."

"No, you're more than that. You're my best friend."

"I think Belvedere might contest that statement."

"He might," she replied. "Can't a woman have two best friends?"

"I don't see why not," Jameson said, leaning closer to her. Before their lips connected for a kiss, he wanted her to know one thing. "May, I intend to use every resource available to me to locate the twins. We will find them and bring them home safely."

"I believe in you, Jameson," May whispered against his lips, then kissed him lightly. Laying her head in the crook of his neck and shoulder, she said on a sleepy yawn, "We will find Donnell and Dour. Your determination is one of the many attributes I love about you."

"Many attributes?" he teased in the form of a question. It warmed his heart to hear her say she loved something about him. Now if he could just get her to love all of him.

"Yes," she answered sleepily. "You are a man of infinite wonders."

Jameson smiled, reaching for her empty glass and setting it on the end table. One day, he hoped to show her how he felt. Unfortunately, tonight was not that night.

Chapter Seven

When the van finally stopped, Cait jerked upright. How long had she been asleep? Where was she? The slam of the doors rocked the vehicle and made her jump. Footsteps on gravel could be heard walking away. Oh God! It hadn't been a bad dream. She really was being held hostage.

"Are ye okay?" he asked.

She shifted her head from side to side, trying to stretch the kink out of her neck. "Yeah. Just a bit stiff."

Donnell handed her clothes to her and she dressed quickly. She couldn't believe she'd fallen asleep in his arms. There went her brilliant plan to weaken his defenses with sex and question him. Then again, she did stay up all night the night before following the idiot of a lead that had gotten them into this predicament. A body might get tired after an all-nighter, not to mention she'd topped it off with a bout of phenomenal sex with a man who claimed to be cursed. She cut a slanted gaze his way before snapping her head toward a noise.

Voices echoed in the distance, softly at first but growing louder as they got closer. The sound of many footsteps followed. The grind of the lift lowering at the rear of the van made her skin crawl. It marked the impending moment of facing the leader of their captors.

She lifted her arm to shield against the bright floodlight filling the cargo space. She blinked to focus. The sight that fell upon her eyes made her gasp. A rather large, barrel-chested man with scraggly red hair stood directly in front of the door. Behind him stood two of the men who had taken them captive. On one side of the redheaded man's head, the hair looked as if it had been scorched in a fire. The hair on one arm was missing and the skin seemed singed, with an angry red hue on his forearm. One of his eyebrows was gone as well, giving him a very strange, yet scary appearance.

The fact he made no effort to hide his face made Cait ill at ease. Did that mean he meant to kill them? She stood and squared off with the man. There was no way she was going to make this easy for them. She held her chin tilted and refused to let the redheaded man's menacing stare shake her.

"I demand to know what's going on." Cait hoped the nervousness twisting her insides didn't sound in her voice. She felt the heat of Donnell behind her and knew he had her back, which gave her a bit of strength to face this redheaded goon.

The platform rose with him on it. He clasped her waist, lifted her as if she weighed nothing, turned and dropped her off the side of the platform. It wasn't a far distance so she managed to land on her feet, but not before her cell phone bounced free of her pocket. Before she could grab it, one of the bad guys stepped on it, shattering any hope of contacting help. She turned her glare on the asshole who'd tossed her off the lift. He glared at her and growled in a thick Scottish brogue, "You'll be learning nuttin' from me."

Donnell plowed into the man, took him completely unawares and knocked him off balance. The man flailed his arms, trying to grapple for a hold on something as he fisted Donnell's kilt. They both fell off the lift, landing in a heap at Cait's feet. She jumped back. Quickly, Donnell pushed up and straddled the man before he could move.

"Ye don't treat a lady like that. Don't ever touch her again," Donnell threatened as he gripped the man's shirt with one hand and poised the other to strike if necessary.

"Whatcha going to do about it?" the man spat as he struggled to punch Donnell.

In a move that would've wowed an audience at a wrestling match, the burned man managed to dislodge Donnell. They sprang to their feet, swinging at one another.

The man hit Donnell square on the cheek, opening a cut under his eye. He didn't even stumble. The blow was hard and would've knocked over a normal person. Donnell was far from the norm. He didn't falter. Instead, he puffed his chest and squared off, taunting his opponent.

"*Mi piuthar*—sister—hits harder than ye do." The pair was close to the same height but the bad guy was much stockier than Donnell. The others gathered around, egging on the fight, spouting obscenities and placing bets on who would win—the man they called Roy or Donnell.

Cait took the opportunity of this distraction to look around for anything she could use as a weapon. She hurriedly backed her way to the front of the van. What she was going to do, she had no idea. If she made it into the driver's seat, she might be able to use the van to threaten to run over the group. Donnell could jump in and they'd make their escape. It was a flimsy plan at best but it was all she had for the moment. Her hand didn't make it to the door handle before a fireball shot across the hood and exploded. Cait stumbled backward and fell onto her derriere.

A person dressed in the garb of a monk limped toward the van. The dusky skies of early morning haloed his head, giving him a spooky, emissary-of-death appeal. The only body part showing was his bony hands. His fingertips glowed. Remembering what the guy at the bar had shared with her, Cait guessed the man beneath the robe had to be Brother Leod. Her informant insisted this Leod person had an arsenal of tricks he used to convince his followers he had magical powers. One of these being he somehow managed to produce fire from his hands.

If this Brother Leod weren't crazy, she'd find that interesting if he wanted to be a magician instead of ridding the world of the MacKinnon brothers and seizing control of some mythical book of black magic spells. All this she wasn't sure she'd believed at the bar but seeing this magical monk wannabe in person put a bit of reality in her current surreal situation.

When she jumped up, spun around and hurried toward Donnell, several men were restraining him and wouldn't let her too close. Now along with a growing bruise on the side of his face and a cut under his eye from earlier, he was sporting a bloody lip. She never saw anyone move as fast as the oversized goon named Roy. Roy was at the monk's side immediately. The leader from the warehouse stood stoic beside the rear of the van with a gun pointed at Donnell. From the looks of

Roy's face, Donnell had gotten in a few decent punches.

The monk didn't get close enough for Cait to get a good look at him. The hood hid his face. His voice sounded weak and gravelly. "Take them to the holding cell."

The hooded men jumped at the command and were ushering them toward what looked like a huge mound rising from the earth. Cait and Donnell both tried to resist. The leader from the warehouse stepped in front of them and landed a hefty blow to Donnell's gut with his one good hand. His other hand was clutched to his chest, obviously severely discolored and swollen from being broken by wheelchair guy at the warehouse. Donnell tried desperately to break free of the men holding him.

"Ye coward," Donnell spat. "Face me in a fair fight and see if ye win."

With a maniacal laugh, the man pulled the gun from where he'd tucked it in his waistband and hit Donnell in the side of the jaw with the butt of it. Donnell's head snapped to one side before it hung low and he shook it as if trying to gain his bearings. Cait broke away from her captors and cupped his face in her hands. Blood dripped from the corner of his mouth and his gaze had a dazed and confused look, much like a boxer's after several rounds in the ring. She turned and took a step toward the crazed monk.

"I want a word with you, Leod," she demanded. "I want to know why we are here and what you plan to do with us." A pair of strong hands banded above her elbows from behind immediately halted her.

The monk's head lifted but the dark kept most of his face concealed within the hood. All she saw was a sinister smile right before he turned and limped toward another large mound. Roy kept pace at his side. He opened a hidden door. Light poured out, showing what appeared to be some sort of underground bunker. Before she got a better look, she and Donnell were shoved in the opposite direction.

The bright floodlights gave Cait enough light to see the area a little more clearly. She saw several more mounds located at regular intervals across the distance. Where the hell were they? Some kind of mole man community? She didn't get much of a chance to look around before one of the men opened a hidden door in the side of the mound. The light from within made her blink. Three men stood inside the narrow hallway, waiting for them to enter.

Their escorts handed them over and slammed the door closed.

"Where are we?" Donnell asked. His words were slurred and Cait was worried he'd been severely injured by that last blow. No one answered. One man simply shoved him. Donnell rose to his full height and glared at the smaller person, who backed off, then fell into step behind a man carrying a metal ring loaded with keys. It amazed Cait that he could walk, much less hold himself upright and stare down a man.

Cait hurried to keep pace. She doubted the guy bringing up the rear would've let her linger. As it was, he was following a little too close for comfort. She swung her arms as she walked, bringing them farther and farther back each time until one fist made contact with his crotch. The direct hit instantly got her point across without a word being exchanged. He gasped as he cupped himself. She shot him a warning glare over her shoulder and he didn't move again until there were several long strides between them.

From the gradual declining slope, he knew they were going underground. The temperature decreased and it seemed as if the corridor never ended. Or it could just be because his head spun with every step, upsetting his orientation. He dug deep for the strength to hide his discomfort. It wouldn't do to let his enemies know they'd injured him even the slightest bit. He attempted to stretch his jaw but the shooting pain stopped him from trying. Licking his lip, he tasted blood. In a fair fight, that never would've happened. He snorted.

Donnell hated not being in control of the situation. There was so much he didn't know. So many questions. When they finally reached the end of the corridor, they stopped and the man in the lead sifted through the keys until he found the right one, inserted it and opened the door.

It pushed inward, showing a large, circular room. Once inside, the door was closed and locked behind them. Something brown and soft covered the floor. To him it looked like a huge pelt. Bright magical lights hung from the ceiling. The walls were made of dirt with wooden beams and supports outlining them. A U-shaped sofa was in the center of the room with a round wooden table in the middle of it. A deck of cards was sorted into three hands. Obviously, the men had been gaming prior to retrieving them.

Donnell counted three more doors distanced perfectly apart from one another around the room. The leader walked to the door directly across from where they entered. The other two maintained a vigilant stance behind him and Cait. Donnell did his best not to show how much it disturbed him to be so out of his element, not only in place but also in time. He sensed these men were dangerous and he'd need every faculty he possessed if he was to keep his promise to Cait.

"Welcome to your new home," the man behind Donnell said. He flicked something on the wall and a light came on.

The guy gave a hard shove in between Donnell's shoulder blades, sending him stumbling into the room. Cait entered quickly behind him. He gained control before falling and turned around in time to see the door slammed shut. The sound of the lock resonated and his gut twisted. He definitely didn't like the caged feeling flowing in his veins. Anger brewed at his inability to fix this situation but he forced it to a simmer. Cait needed him to be strong and not an anger-driven idiot unable to think straight. If he succeeded, his *brathair* Gavin would be proud.

For a second, his *brathair*'s image flashed behind his eyes. Fear of not knowing what happened to his family clenched his heart but he waged a battle to contain it. Escape and keeping Cait safe was what he should be focused on, not the past and the long-gone people from it.

With the substantial spin of his brains, it was impossible to focus. There had to be a way out of this. He steadied himself as his gaze fell upon a scared, trembling creature and his heart sank. Though she put on a brave front, he sensed she was anything but. Taking a breath, he concentrated on Cait. He wanted to help her. He did his best to sound calm and aimed to soothe her angst even though his jaw hurt and his head ached.

"Are ye okay?"

"Yeah," Cait replied, "just pissed off." She gently touched his chin and shook her head. "We've got to get your wounds cleaned." She turned to the sink in the far corner. A towel and a washcloth lay neatly on the shelf above it. "Let me wet one of those, then we can take care of you."

Donnell snorted. The woman had spirit. He liked that. When she sat on the only cot in the room, he lowered to the floor at her feet and got comfortable.

She cupped his chin and gently touched the cloth to his bloody lip, then carefully brushed it along the cut under his eye, removing the remnants of the fight. He tried not to grimace even though it hurt each time she swiped the cloth to his wounds. "You're going to have a nasty bruise, but I don't think the cut needs stitches. Any wider and it would've."

He grinned as an image popped into his head. "I like the way ye dispensed of the idiot following a wee bit too closely in the hallway."

Her face brightened and her eyebrows rose as if surprised. "You saw that?"

"Aye." He nodded. Covering the front of his kilt with his hands, he teased, "Remind me never to piss ye off, as ye say."

He liked the sound of her laughter as she let loose. Donnell was pleased he'd given her a moment of happiness during this drearily taxing event.

Cait wiped the water from her eyes as she sobered. "With the prize you have between your thighs, you needn't worry about me hurting it." Her eyes widened and he knew she hadn't meant to let it slip just how much she'd enjoyed their coupling.

He inched closer. "So ye think my shaft to be a prize, do ye?"

A flush of light red filled her cheeks as a sensual smile crossed her lips. Lips he wanted to kiss. "Aye. Yours is worthy of a blue ribbon."

He leaned in, readying to take that kiss. "Blue ribbon?"

"First place. The best of the best," she replied right before his lips met hers.

Cait's mouth tasted sweeter than he remembered from earlier. Granted, he'd savored the flavor of her sheath and planned to sample it again, but her kiss ignited his lust in a way no other wench ever did. She returned the pressure of their connection, lip on lip, tongue twisted with tongue, driving him crazy. He wanted more even though his jaw was tender and sore. Kissing her wouldn't be enough to shave even a sliver from the intense need growing in him for this woman. No amount of pain would stop him from enjoying her kiss.

He had to touch her bosom. It made him smile against her mouth when she guided his hands directly where he had wanted them in the first place, as if she had a magical insight into his mind. For a split second a thought speared his brain. Was she a witch? It was instantly washed away when she cupped his bawls. Her aim was precise, even through the thick kilt. Her expertise in rolling them carefully, but with enough pressure to shift him into a solid rod in a matter of moments had him moaning in delight.

"*Och*," he groaned, pulling from their kiss. "Ye be the master of my shaft. Cait, I need to be between your legs."

The sexy smile that split her lips made him even hungrier for her. She stood, straddling him since he was so close to the cot she had little room to maneuver. He had no intention of giving her any space as he helped her out of her clothes. With each item removed, he tasted her flesh, kissing and nipping a delightful trail directly to her sheath. He grasped her buttocks, kneading the supple fleshy globes in his hands as his tongue speared between her folds, delving for her hidden bud.

"Mi brèagha neamhnaid," he whispered breathily against her clit then licked it, suckling it between his lips, tugging until she moaned his name.

Donnell shoved his finger into her heat and found it perfect. He looked at her as he nuzzled her mound. "Ye are as ready for me as I am ready for ye."

He bunched his kilt around his waist, revealing his shaft pointed heavenward. Carefully, he guided Cait into position and held her poised for entrance. He kept his eyes on hers, watching her face as she lowered, taking him into her until she was fully seated on his lap. Her pupils dilated with desire and her eyes brightened with heat as he set a slow pace.

The way Cait rocked on his shaft sent intense shock waves to his bawls, tightening them into a constricted sac, desperately in need of release. *Och*, the lass knew how to control his pleasure. Each movement drew him to the edge only to keep him hovering, wanting for more until she was ready to shove him into the abyss and not one second before she deemed it to happen. Donnell buried his face between the haven of her luscious breasts. Aye, he loved a full-bosomed woman and Cait's were the right size for him. Plump, round nipples suitable to suckle and full of flesh to nuzzle his face between. Cait's were the picture of perfection to him.

Donnell held her breasts in his hands, enjoying the way they danced as she rode him. He bobbed from one nipple to the other, toying and tasting, flicking the points with his tongue and loving her subtle gasps of joy. He could do this all night, but he knew he wouldn't last. Not with the way her sheath massaged his taut flesh with every stroke, every sensual shift. Her pace increased and her nails dug into his shoulders.

He released the wondrous globes he cherished and gripped her waist. The lass was close to release and so was he. He speared into her over and over, sweat trickling down his spine. The tease of her nipples doing a bounce-and-swirl sort of thing in his face was more than he could bear. Donnell latched on to one nipple and tugged it hard with his teeth. Cait squealed in delight and shivered from head to toe as the rush of pleasure rolled over her, taking them both over the edge. His shaft shook, releasing his essence, combining it with hers as it coated his flesh. Nothing felt more heavenly than a satisfied woman in his arms, especially this woman.

Donnell's face was pressed against her breasts as she clung to him. A rush of phenomenal sensations flooded him, stirring his emotions to a new height. He held her close, breathing her scent, taking his fill. He'd had women before and he'd given as much as he'd taken. With Cait it was different. The thought burrowed itself deep in his brain and wouldn't let go. He liked resting inside her. The tremors of her sheath coaxing every last drop of his essence from his shaft until his bawls were but a fleshy sac between his thighs. Being with Cait gave him a moment of peace in this awakening to a new world, a one he knew naught about.

Though he liked where he was, he knew it couldn't last. Not if they didn't escape this prison. He kissed his way from the valley between her bosoms to her neck, to her jaw, then tenderly touched her lips.

"Milady, though this be heavenly, we need to devise a plan of escape."

"Aye," she conceded on a hushed breath against his brow. "You're right."

She stretched then slowly stood. Instant cold surrounded his shaft and he regretted their separation but it had to be done. He had no intention of being a prisoner forever. Donnell straightened his kilt and cocked his head to get a better view of Cait as she cleaned herself and dressed. She was a vision of womanly beauty. Full breasts, nice round bottom and a sturdy build strong enough to handle the likes of him, not to mention her sensual brown eyes that hid nothing if one took the time to look. She shot him a coy smile and he couldn't help but smile back. He'd been caught staring and he didn't care.

"Do you not give a lady a moment of privacy to dress?" she teased as she turned her back to him.

"Ye are a feast upon which my eyes shall never get their fill, Cait." Donnell playfully gave her a light slap upon her arse as he laughed. She jumped and gave him a pretend look of shock as she took a step away and continued to dress.

Donnell shifted onto his knees with his hands upon his thighs as if to stand but froze.

An ungodly pain shot through his heart. Heat filled his soul and his skin seemed to burn. Argh. Had his opponent hit him harder than he realized? Something was wrong. He couldn't take a full breath. His chest constricted. His body refused to move and suddenly became lifeless. A pain-filled scream lodged in his throat, then all went dark.

Heat sizzled down Cait's spine and filled the air. She spun around. Fear froze her to the ground. Her eyes widened.

"Holy mother of God," she whispered, stunned by what greeted her gaze.

When she finally found the strength to move, she slowly circled the solid-rock form of Donnell. How could this be? She touched his face, read the pain in his eyes and sensed his distress. Whatever happened hurt him. Anger boiled to the surface. This wasn't right. Who did this to him and how? Why?

Cait stumbled to the cot and landed hard as she sank against the wall. She couldn't take her eyes from the statue of Donnell. One moment he had been this hot, sexy man. The next he was a solid wall of stone.

She closed her eyes and let the tears flow. This was the best and worst night of her life. Confusion spiraled through her thoughts. She and Jenny had tailed a suspect to a warehouse. They saw a crime being committed, then got dragged into a fight. She ended up in a van with a hunk. Had sex with the hunk, *twice*. Now he was an inanimate object.

Ancient words whispered through her brain. She couldn't remember them all, but she remembered it being beautiful. Opening her eyes, she directed her gaze to Donnell. Somehow the old woman freed him from a curse. At least that's how she envisioned it as having happened.

Did she believe in curses?

Looking at the statue, she decided she did. That had to be the only explanation. Now what? She struggled to remember the words spoken that set him free but couldn't. Damn. Did she need to speak them again to break him out of that prison or was it a one-time deal?

Totally confused, she curled into a ball on the cot. Unstoppable tears rushed her. She needed to rest. No. What she needed to do was think but at the moment she couldn't as her thoughts convoluted into a taut bundle of pain that sent short bursts of fiery spikes throughout her head. The forthcoming migraine couldn't be stopped. The events of her night combined with her exhaustion equaled a massive headache. She reached for his hand, hoping he was somehow alive in that strange stone prison. The light became too much to bear and she lost the battle to keep her eyes open.

Cait dug out a pill she always tucked in the tiny pocket within the front pocket of her jeans. She hated to take it but if she didn't and the migraine persisted, she'd never work out a plan of escape for them. She moved to the sink, palmed some water and downed the medication. Grabbing a towel, she lay on the cot and covered her eyes. Not sure if she did it hoping to comfort the man cursed to stone or for herself, she kept her hand on his. It was best to let the medication take effect if she wanted to get anything accomplished.

Silently she prayed. *Please keep Donnell safe.* She lay still and waited for sleep.

Donnell couldn't move. His mind was fully awake but his body failed him. He knew both eyes were open but no sight filled them, only darkness. Cait? Was she near? Had the same befallen her? No. He felt it had not. This was the curse that had taken his family. Somehow he understood this to be true. Dour. Had he been stricken as well? He prayed not. If one of them was to remain free, he hoped it had been his *brathair*. Digging deep, he tapped into that special connection he had with his twin and sensed the same had happened to Dour.

How? Why?

He'd been freed then recaptured by its solid tomb walls once again. What had he done to deserve such treatment? Donnell struggled with the issues. Though he willed his body to move, it refused. He could take no air into his lungs but somehow he didn't need any at the moment. Every part of him sat motionless in this eerie location, hovering between life and death.

Would death be better? The thought toyed with his consciousness. Was this how he was to remain? Awake but trapped, unable to move, listening to those around him without the ability to speak or respond? His rapidly fired questions skidded to a halt.

Could he hear someone outside his prison? Donnell strained to listen, hoping at least that part of his body functioned. He inwardly cringed. Cait's soft whimper reached him and he ached to soothe her angst. She cried. He tried desperately to move, to brush away her fears, but his hands would not respond. His lips refused to say the words that wove through his thoughts.

This was not good. She was alone. Anger brewed but there was naught he could do. He could not protect her locked inside here. Donnell attempted to flex his muscles, to expand his cage but nothing happened. He couldn't even grit his teeth in frustration or ball his fists. He wished for her safety and prayed to the gods to keep her from harm.

If any of the gods in the heavens be listening, please keep this wee lass out of harm's way. She deserves no pain at the cost of knowing me.

Her image floated behind his eyes. He'd tasted her, sampled her womanly gifts and hungered for more. *Och.* Was this how he was to spend eternity? Wanting a woman he could never have again? A woman with perfect breasts that jiggled when she laughed and teased him when she rode him. For a second he relished the beauty of her face when she reached her pleasure. Aye. That was a vision he prayed to see again. If not, then he hoped this one memory never faded and kept him company until his mind finally quit and he found peace within this strange resting place.

If his mouth worked he'd love to savor her flavor upon his tongue. He liked the feel of her hidden pearl between his fingertips when he rolled it to bring her joy. That subtle intake of air she took each time he licked it then sucked it, increasing her desire. If his shaft could respond, he knew just thinking of sex with Cait would have him hard and ready for her sheath. A sheath he knew fit around him nicely. Snug, tight and wet. Just the way he liked his Cait to be.

His Cait? Donnell paused.

The woman was not his to claim, *especially* not in his current condition. Images of Cait traipsed through his mind. His desire for her increased and tormented him. He knew he could not have her. This magnificent woman would not be his to kiss, to hold. He longed to be nestled between her luscious thighs and share the release of their mutual essences mixing together within her heat. Aye. Now there was a thought that brought him momentary gladness. If his lips worked, he'd be smiling, thinking of Cait.

Donnell focused on the woman he'd known for the span of a night. No other came into the center of his thoughts. Thinking of her brought him peace. A peace he prayed would see him through however many years he'd be trapped alive but dead within the limits of this curse.

Chapter Eight

Jenny kept her distance and had even followed the van without using headlights for the last hour. The road they traveled was desolate, with little traffic flow in the wee morning hours. She hoped that by extinguishing her headlights the driver of the van would think the car turned onto a side road. That was if he even had noticed them at all. With Dour as her navigator, they'd kept a great deal of distance between them and focused only on the van's red taillights as their beacon in the dark. Luckily, she had enough moonlight to keep the car on the road.

Out of the corner of her eye, she noticed he'd managed to relax into the seat and had even loosened the intense grip he'd held on the dashboard for most of the ride. From the white color of his knuckles, she'd half expected his handprints to be forever embedded in the dash.

He'd been filled with questions and she'd done her best to answer them. Most were about the car. Typical guy questions, how'd it work, what did the steering wheel do, the radio, the gearshift, the dashboard, how did the window operate, and most importantly what did it eat? That last one made her laugh.

Then she'd realized he was comparing it to what he knew — horses. After that, she tried to see things more from his confused perspective. How would she feel if she'd been awakened from a curse after a couple of centuries? Deciding she'd be scared shitless, she thought his questions through more carefully and held her laughter so as not to discourage him from learning about this new world.

When the van turned and stopped at a guarded gate, Jenny pulled the car off the road and waited. She didn't want to drive past and be seen so she chose the first accessible location to hide and watch — a grove of trees. The moonlight filtered through the branches. Each crunch under the tires made her stomach sink as she hoped she wasn't doing any damage to the car. Cait would kill her. She parked as deeply in the underbrush as she could without getting the car stuck and without hitting a tree.

"Stay here," she commanded Dour. Carefully, she climbed out through the open window so the inside light wouldn't come on if she opened the door. This wouldn't have been an issue if the switch on the light worked and she could've turned it off and gotten out through the door. The car was old and several things no longer worked.

Catching sight of movement in the car, she leaned back inside and spoke on a hurried whisper to Dour. "Don't get out. I'm getting Cait's binoculars."

"*Mi brathair* be in trouble and ye want me to do nothing?" he grumbled and she could tell he wasn't happy about being told what to do. She wasn't sure if he didn't like being told what to do or that it came from a woman.

"For the moment, yes," she commanded in a low tone, trying not to lose her temper. "We need to think this through and not act on impulse or it might get them killed."

She waited until he reluctantly agreed. Jenny turned and walked to the trunk. The moment she opened it, a bright flash at the compound stunned her and she immediately focused on the van, searching for any sign of Cait. Being too far away to see much, she prayed Cait and Dour's brother were safe.

"What happened?" Dour questioned as he hung as far out as the passenger window allowed.

She would've openly laughed at the sight of such a large man squeezing out such a small hole if they weren't in such a predicament. For a second, she wished she hadn't shown him how to roll the window down in the first place. Was he stuck? She hoped he wasn't.

Good thing she didn't show him how to open the door. With the way he listened to her, he'd probably be storming the enemy by now without a plan of attack and blowing any possibility of saving Cait and Donnell.

"Not sure," she answered as she hurriedly retrieved the binocular case, opened it and scoured the area with the binoculars. She got a glimpse of Cait and Dour's brother being shoved toward a doorway into what looked like a hill. Was it some sort of underground facility? Jenny shook her head. How in the hell was she going to get her friend out of there? "It looked like some sort of explosion."

Had Cait used that firecracker she kept in her emergency kit? Nah. It was too big an explosion for a single firecracker. It had to be something else.

"What do ye see?" he questioned impatiently, causing the car to rock a little as he tried his best to reposition. Jenny moved toward the passenger side and prayed he didn't turn the car over with his efforts.

"Not sure," she replied, letting go of the binoculars so they hung around her neck. "They've been taken into some sort of odd-shaped building. Could you stop trying to get out through the window? You're not going to fit and you just might turn over the car. Then where would we be? I'll tell you," she stated sternly, not wanting to yell at him in case her voice echoed and somehow reached the compound. "We'd be without transportation when we free them and make our getaway, that's where."

Dour froze as if contemplating her words. Then the car rocked again as he wiggled himself back inside, grumbling as he went. "If'n this thing turned over, it'd be no trouble to right it with me sheer will."

Jenny ground her teeth, trying to control the need to scream. The pressure of the situation threatened her resolve but she dug for the strength to remain in control. One of them had to be. If it were up to the antique giant, they'd rush the compound and either die trying to save the others or end up locked away with them.

Grabbing a backpack full of emergency supplies and a pair of blankets from the trunk, she returned to the driver's side and handed the items to Dour through the window, then climbed back in.

"Where did ye get these? We are in the beast's, um, car's belly. It looked as if ye pulled these from its mouth?"

Jenny smiled inwardly. The front of the car opening probably did look like a mouth to this ancient Scotsman. "Almost every car has an area to store things called a trunk. In this model, it's located in the front and the engine is in the rear."

"Ah, the engine, the thing that makes the car go," he said. She liked the way his thick Scottish brogue rolled across each word and his childlike wonder only added to his charm.

She shook her head. *Don't go thinking about his charm.* What she needed was a plan. Jenny rifled through the backpack and pulled out a battery-powered lantern. It had four settings — high, medium, low and a very dim nightlight level, which was the one she chose. To keep it from being seen, she pulled the windshield screen from the rear seat and put it in place. She then leaned out the window with the binoculars in hand, trying to scout the area as best as possible.

"From what I saw, they've been taken into an area of hills. What be this place?" Dour asked.

"I've got a feeling it's one of those underground bunker communities."

"Underground bunker communities?" he questioned and it hit her just how much she needed to teach him about this new era. His world was long gone. "It looked to me as if they went into the side of a hill."

"They did," she answered. "I think it probably leads into an underground house of sorts."

"Like a cave?"

If that worked for him, she'd roll with it. "Yeah. Like a cave."

His brother was a prisoner in a van that had just entered a guarded compound. From what little she could see, it looked heavily fortified. It was dark and difficult to judge from this distance, even with the binoculars and the floodlights in the area near the guardhouse.

The way her and Cait's luck had been running lately, they'd probably stumbled upon the very community the authorities had been combing the countryside to locate. Dozens of these types of underground bunkers had been sprouting up, especially in areas known to have been former mining locations. With the bad economy, many people were choosing to go off the grid and disappear into these communities in order to survive. Whole families were moving into these groups and building new lives. Hoarding supplies, relocating and prepping as if the world were coming to an end. It was a little too creepy in her opinion.

According to a recent news report, a gang was suspected to have infiltrated one of these compounds and taken it over. But authorities weren't able to find it. So far it was mere speculation by the media. Looking around at the barbed wire and the occasional shadow of a person perusing the perimeter, she'd bet money it wasn't a figment of some overzealous reporter's imagination. Nope. Her gut instinct screamed they'd landed in a bad situation instead of a group of harmless families trying to survive.

She handed him the binoculars. "You can get a better look if you use these."

After a few moments of helping him adjust them to his eyes, she leaned back in the seat. Her eyes hurt from what she saw. What was she going to do and how was she going to get Cait out of there alive? They didn't have any training for something like this. Hell, they were paranormal journalists, not gangland survivalists. Those guys had guns. She and Cait didn't. Her heart pounded and her stomach churned. This wasn't good.

Should she try to pull the car out of their hiding spot and drive back to the nearest town for help? What if they saw her? Would they chase after them and catch them before they reached help? Her head ached from the bevy of questions torturing her thoughts.

It'd been a while since she'd checked the cell phone for service. Maybe she'd get lucky and could call for help, otherwise she had no idea what they were going to do. Jenny flipped onto her knees and leaned between the seats, trying to find the device she'd tossed in the backseat in a moment of frustration. She found it, shot upright and hit her head.

"Damn," she grumbled in pain.

Dour caught her as she clumsily attempted to return to her seat. His warm hands circled her slender waist and steadied her. Holding the phone where she could see it, she saw there was still no signal. It was the last straw. She flopped into his lap, landed hard on the binoculars and started to cry. The events of the night overwhelmed her. She and Cait had done a lot of crazy things but nothing as dangerous as this, nothing that meant the difference between life and death.

"Your brother and my best friend are hostages," she gasped between sobs. "I have no clue how to save them and no way to call for help." She leaned into him, letting the tears fall as she curled into a ball in his lap.

He wiggled the binoculars out from under her and placed them on what Jenny had explained to him earlier was the dash. The lass had a right to cry. *Och.* If he weren't a man, he'd be crying as well. Life had taken a truly odd turn. One minute he'd been sleeping off a drunken night. The next he was brushing stone and dirt from his face, being told he'd been cursed, getting into a brawl and losing his *brathair* to a creature called a van. Now he was holding a crying woman.

If he weren't so damn confused, having a beautiful woman in his arms would be a fine turn of events. Had he really been cursed? Considering where he was at the moment, trapped in a thing called a car that ran without horses, being cursed was the only answer.

He doubted their older *brathairs* had gone to such elaborate lengths to pull a prank on them as they had so many times before on their elders, especially on Ian. Swapping out Ian's favorite handmade quivers for some he and Donnell made cost Ian a prize buck and almost earned them a firm hand from Gavin. Instead, they'd mucked stables for a week, even though Gavin thought it a fine lesson for Ian. He should've checked his weapons before the hunt. The memory brought Dour a moment of joy.

The lass shifted in his lap, bringing him back to reality. He couldn't help but inhale her scent. Her hair smelled of strawberries. He liked strawberries. Dour breathed deeply. The odor was the most pleasant thing he'd smelled in a while. He frowned. If what he'd been told was right, that *while* equaled over two hundred years.

He cradled Jenny closer, trying to soothe her angst and his own in the process. His chest tightened and he knew his world was no longer as he remembered. Looking at the item she clutched, it was cell phones and cars and God knew what else he'd have to learn in order to acclimate with his surroundings. Maybe this was all just a strange dream spurned on by a bad batch of ale.

Dour closed his eyes tight, praying things would be normal. Strawberry essence filled his nose and he knew exactly what he'd see. A beautiful woman stuck in a strange situation with him. How bad could it be? He and his *brathair* had been in tight spots before and they'd always managed to muddle their way through the mire.

This was just another one of those times. At least that's what he tried to convince himself. He leaned his head against the window and stared at the stars. *Ye fates have given me and mi brathair an odd path to follow.* He sighed heavily, closed his eyes and prayed for his family. Were any of them alive? Had they all been cursed? Not knowing the answers tightened the constriction in his chest. The one person who might help them was the older redhead who told them they'd been cursed in the first place.

His eyes widened as he stroked Jenny's hair while she cried. The older woman knew their names. How? She had to know about their family, their clan.

A slow smile upturned his lips as a plan formulated. First, break Donnell out of that compound, as Jenny had called it. Second, find the redhead. He looked at the sky, judging the time 'til daylight. Maybe an hour at best. At first light, he planned to sneak as close as possible to the area and determine the easiest way in. Then wait until dusk, slip inside, find Donnell and escape. In his head it sounded simple. In reality, he doubted it'd be as straightforward. Even the best-laid plans faltered from time to time and he didn't expect anything less.

When a firm bottom wiggled in his lap, his thoughts instantly shifted to Jenny. His chest was damp from her tears. He had hardened with every subtle movement of her luscious arse. She'd given him a perfect view of it when she'd leaned into the back to retrieve the phone. It'd only taken her a couple of seconds to find it but the eyeful she'd given him had been a delightful treat. In a different scenario, he might have acted upon such an open invitation with a playful swat upon it to fire her desire. But he'd refrained. It was the gentlemanly thing to do, given the situation they were in.

Gently he stroked the back of her head and wished she didn't feel so phenomenal in his arms. His eyes widened when she placed tender kisses to his neck, then his chin and lastly connected with his mouth. Somewhere in the back of his mind a little voice was screaming, *The lass be in distress. This no be the time for sex. Comfort her.* His body wasn't listening.

Dour increased the firmness of his lips to hers, sucking her tongue and enjoying her flavor. He knew he should stop but couldn't. Part of him wanted to know if his shaft still functioned. After all, it'd been quite a long time, if his having been cursed was to be believed.

Jenny broke from the kiss and frantically pulled off her shirt. When she reached behind her and unhooked the silky piece of clothing binding her breasts, they sprang free for his enjoyment. He couldn't help but smile at the precious sight. Two perfect globes sat waiting for him to sample. And taste he did. Dour fondled the handfuls, flicking the nipples with his tongue until she moaned.

"I need you," she gasped as she fumbled with her pants.

Why a woman wore a man's *trews*, he did not understand, but she looked strikingly attractive in them. He helped her as best he could in the confines of the small car. After a few head bumps, an elbow hard to the window and a gearshift in her hip, their struggle ended and she was naked. Long lean legs straddled his lap and he ran his hands along her thighs.

"Ye are beautiful, lass."

"Thank you," Jenny gasped, attempting to tug the front of his kilt up around his waist. He lifted, allowing more movement in the fabric, and she bumped her head on the roof again since she sat on his lap. She commanded, "Dour, press your feet into the floor."

He did as instructed just as she leaned for something between the lower edge of the seat and the door. The seat slid back with a thud, then lay almost flat, giving him more legroom to maneuver. It wasn't much, but the slender woman on his lap utilized it perfectly. She repositioned until her knees were beside his hips and his kilt was rolled into a bunch at his waist. She froze and he followed her stare.

His shaft stood hard, straight and ready. In slow motion, she caressed him from base to tip. He liked the feel of her hands and the way they gracefully danced along his skin. He couldn't take his eyes off her long, thin fingers as they cared for him. If she kept this up, he'd reach his pleasure within a matter of minutes. Dour wanted to be inside her.

"Jenny." He spoke her name on a haggard breath. Her eyes met his and he didn't have to say another word. It was as if she knew his very thoughts.

He steadied her by holding on to her narrow waist as she guided him home. Never had a woman's sheath felt as magnificent as Jenny's did the moment he breached her opening and she slowly sank onto him, taking him in all the way to the hilt. She arched and he grasped her hips, giving her the support she needed to ride him. He liked this position of a woman in command of her pleasure. Given their location, he doubted they could accomplish this any other way. With the limited room, Dour's muscles contracted.

Och. Now wasn't the time for his legs to cramp.

She couldn't believe her reaction to Dour at a time like this. It had to be the intense stress of the situation driving her to sexually attack a complete stranger. She couldn't stop. She wanted him. No. She needed him to comfort her. She tried desperately to justify her actions. The feel of him against her as she'd cried ignited her senses, making her even more aware of his sexuality. His build wasn't that of one of those weightlifters or physique builders. It appeared earned through everyday life, chopping wood and hunting, surviving in elements through the sheer will to live.

Ugh. Jenny chided herself. She couldn't stop her eyes from soaking in every glorious inch of him. Wild red hair hung scattered about his shoulders, taunting her fingertips with its silkiness. Penetrating green eyes stared directly at her. His chest was broad, as were his biceps. He looked incredibly large crammed into the front seat of this small car. Still he held her, easing her distress at the expense of his own comfort.

Stress-induced lust, that's why this was happening. She tried to put an acceptable spin on it as she rode Dour. Her breathing increased and the sexual tension swirled into a tightly wound spring ready to explode at any moment with every delicious stroke of him in and out of her. Pounding down on him almost pushed her over the edge but instead she dangled, hanging on by a thin thread of ecstasy.

"*Och*," Dour groaned and twisted, bucking her wildly, causing her to lose her balance. His fingers dug into her hips. She grabbed his shoulders for support but still banged her temple on the glass. Damn. Stars shot behind her eyes as he speared into her at an odd angle. Pain mixed with pleasure and that was all she needed. Invisible scissors cut the thin string and she spiraled into the abyss. A slight throb in her head was nothing compared to the orgasm racing through her at the moment.

Jenny shivered from the intensity of the sensations flooding her. She leaned against him, gasping for a deep breath. She didn't get more than a moment to loll in the afterglow.

"Lass," he panted. The grimace on his face couldn't be mistaken for anything other than pain. "I need to be standing. My legs are tightening."

"Oh," she said as she awkwardly slid off him and sideways into the driver's seat. "You've got a cramp." She reached across him and opened the car door while she shielded the overhead light with a blanket.

He practically rolled out of the car as if he were a pistachio nut being pried from a shell.

Somehow he managed to land on his feet in a crouched position. She kept the blanket over the light until he eased around the door and closed it, extinguishing the lamp. Even though it was becoming lighter as sunrise approached, Jenny didn't want to take any chances of being caught by the brighter light somehow being seen. She turned off the lantern since it was no longer needed to see.

Dour slowly stood and she sensed from his cautious movements he scoured the area for signs of intruders. His muscles bunched and flexed as he stretched. He moved in a circular pattern around the car, keeping his back to her, reinforcing her thought that he was on the lookout. Carefully, she got out of the car, carrying her clothes. She stretched then dressed as he stood watch.

Jenny stepped into her panties and her jeans, then in a practiced move had her bra on in a second. She lifted her shirt to put it on over her head as she asked, "How are your legs feeling?"

As she tugged the shirt onto her head, an electrified tingle filled the air, coated her bared flesh and slithered down her spine. "Jenny." Her name whispered in agony had her quickly popping her head through the shirt's opening only to stop dead still and stare. Her jaw hung open and her eyes widened.

Dour stood at the front of the car, frozen in stone. The sun's rays filtered through the trees and haloed him in a beam of light. Out of habit, she finished putting on her shirt. Her feet moved of their own accord in his direction. She rubbed her eyes, hoping it was some sort of trick and blinked, but it didn't change. Dour was a statue once again. Her fingers trembled and she wasn't sure if she should touch him, but had to know if this was real.

He was on his feet, back straight with a slight twist at the waist where he had turned to look in her direction when he spoke her name. One arm was outstretched as if he'd reached for her before this wicked curse claimed him again. Jenny's fingers hovered within mere inches of touching his cheek.

Was this the curse? If so, how did it happen, hadn't the old woman in the warehouse freed them? Question after question tumbled through her head. Now what the hell was she going to do? She paced around him, letting her fingers touch him ever so lightly, hoping without hope this was a weird dream and she'd wake soon to find herself in her bedroom in the flat she shared with Cait.

Something caught her eye and she switched to panic mode. Her brain whirled and she sprang into action. For a split second, the silver window shield reflected the sun when a breeze whispered through the trees, moving the limbs that hung low over the car. She couldn't have that happen again. Jenny reached in through the window and jerked the shield from its place. Quickly she folded it and tucked it into the backseat. Not sure how much was visible from this grove of trees and underbrush to the compound, she decided not to take any risk.

She grabbed the forest-green blanket and laid it across the car, covering as much of the hood and windshield as possible. She gathered a couple of downed branches and laid them on the roof and leaned them against the rear, being careful to spread them for maximum coverage. As fast and as neatly as possible, she did her best to cover the car's tracks leading into the trees. Lastly, she covered Dour with the dark-brown blanket. Now if anyone scanned this area, she hoped nothing stood out too drastically that they'd send someone over to investigate.

Jenny used the binoculars. The compound seemed quiet. From what she saw, the guardhouse contained two people. The gate was kept closed. There were at least eight mounds, signifying underground bunkers to her. There could be more. Her heart sank. What was she going to do? She looked at Dour's lifeless form. She couldn't leave him here and go for help. What if they found him? What would they do to him? Worse, what could she do to stop them? Tiredness made her legs shake as she walked over to him.

Not sure why she did it, she hugged him, wrapping her arms underneath the blanket. Her cheek pressed to the stone center of his chest. A faint sound thumped in her ear and it scared her. She pulled back without releasing her hold to his waist. Was that his heartbeat? Nah, it couldn't be. Just to make sure, she listened again with her ear snugly pressed in the center of his chest. *Thump. Thump.* A steady beat told her he definitely lived inside this strange tomb of sorts.

She stepped back and stared. Without a doubt, this was the oddest case she and Cait had ever dealt with. She glanced in the direction of the compound. And it was the most dangerous. Jenny returned to the car, leaned inside and disconnected the bulb from the overhead light. *Should've thought of that sooner.* Leaving the driver's side door open, she laid the seat back, got as comfortable as possible and ate a protein bar she retrieved from the backpack along with a bottle of water. She'd made fun of Cait for keeping this thing stocked, but now she was damn glad her best friend had the foresight to do so.

Jenny picked up the cell phone and checked for a signal just in case. Nothing, but the battery was getting low. She attached the car charger and plugged it in. Everything ached with tiredness. Her eyes grew heavy as she clutched the phone to her chest and wished for a miracle. Though she was determined to remain focused on the compound, exhaustion won the battle and forced her to succumb to sleep.

Pain shot through Dour's chest and he thought he'd crumple to the ground. Heat sizzled, filling him with the sensation of being on fire for a split second then disappearing, taking his freedom with it. The last thing he saw was Jenny's surprised look as she met his gaze right before darkness surrounded him.

How could this be? Wasn't he free from the curse? Dour struggled to break from the solid wall that bound him. Frustration bounced around his brain, threatening his sanity. Nothing responded to his mental commands. His limbs did not obey. His eyes could not see and his mouth did not speak. Yet he had the ability to think and reason.

He willed himself to relax and work out this puzzle contrived of twisted magic. There had to be a reason the curse returned to him. Had it also taken Donnell? Panic threatened his deductive process as an image of his twin locked in stone flashed inside his head. Though he prayed Donnell was free, he instinctively knew the truth. Both he and Donnell were entombed.

Not if he could help it. Dour concentrated on the events of their release. There had to be a logical reason for what happened. What changed? He cataloged his thoughts, trying to deduce an answer.

First he and Donnell were awakened after a two-hundred-year nap by a stunning older redhead. Second they did one of their favorite things, they got in a fight. The memory would've made him snort if he could've as he considered the episode as not much of a brawl. Not like the ones he and his *brathairs*… Dour paused.

Were any of his other *brathairs* free? Had they all been cursed? It saddened him to think the others suffered the same fate as he and Donnell. He prayed they'd enjoyed long, happy lives and mourned the loss of him and Donnell by seeking revenge against the person behind this curse. He struggled to clear his thoughts of his family. One by one, their faces flashed behind his eyes. Gavin. Ian. Padon. Struan. Aiden. And his one and only *piuthar* — sister — Akira.

What became of them? The woman hadn't mentioned any of his *brathairs* when she freed them. Then again, she didn't have much of a chance to tell them anything. They'd been tossed right into the middle of a brawl.

Dour desperately tried to clear his thoughts of his loved ones' images. It tormented his soul, knowing he'd never see them again. He needed his mind focused on the current issue if he was to determine the way to true freedom for him and Donnell.

What if there was no path to freedom? What if the one night was all they got? Dour shook those delinquent thoughts from his mind. He refused to retreat into the negative and suffer the mental torture of being awake yet asleep at the same time. Then it struck him.

The one night.

That was the difference. They had been awakened at night.

The woman claimed she set them free. He worked through what she'd said. *There were constraints.* What sort of constraints did she mean? She would not have stated she'd set them free if she hadn't. Would she have? They didn't know her. What if she lied? Dour studied her words in his head. No. The way she'd spoken to him and Donnell was with such conviction, such honesty, she believed she'd given them a way to freedom.

Yet, one with constraints.

Constraints. That word tumbled through his brain. What sort of ties still wove around this curse keeping them bound? Dour thought back to the moment he'd felt that first tingle. What changed that brought the curse on again? What was he doing when it started? A stroke of the sun's rays brushed his cheek and had him meeting his first sunrise in many years. He'd only gotten a brief glimpse when…

Dour smiled inwardly. The answer beamed as bright as a beacon of sunlight. He was giddy with hope he'd figured out the constraint of which the woman spoke. This freedom came with a restriction. Come nightfall he and Donnell would be free again. That idea sparked a sense of relief and gave him a light at the end of his tunnel. He might be wrong but refused to allow negative thought to overrule his momentary joy.

That sliver of hope was all he had to keep him sane. That and the images of a beautiful woman who traipsed through his mind and gave him something else to think about and enjoy while he waited. Dour liked the vision of Jenny sitting perched on him. He couldn't help but laugh inwardly at the memory of their coupling in that tiny car. Each bumped something somewhere and still they gave each other pleasure. It didn't matter his legs cramped and she'd knocked her head against the roof several times.

Dour struggled to contain the laughter rolling through his mind. Image after image of their difficult first time set his spirits on high. He liked that Jenny was an adventurous woman. The memory of how she felt wrapped around him soothed any lingering angst as he relished the idea of sampling her glorious attributes once again come nightfall. The sensual imagery came to a screeching halt.

Jenny was alone.

This hit him like a solid blow to the jaw in a brawl. This long, lean creature was unattended in a situation of severe danger. What if the people from the compound found her? What if they took her hostage? *No. Don't think like that.* He tried to focus on the good as he prayed for her safety.

She was a smart woman. Jenny would be safe until he woke to help her. This he tried to convince himself was truth. He *would* wake again. It was the only thought that gave him a miniscule amount of hope and that was all he needed to survive. He was determined he'd awaken again at nightfall and have the chance to hold Jenny once again.

He prayed he was right.

Chapter Nine

"Trust me, Draven, you imbecile," Leod stated tersely from behind his desk, knowing the man bristled at being called nothing short of stupid. He did it on purpose to show he didn't fear Draven. "You've brought me a MacKinnon."

The ringleader from the warehouse grumbled in return, "How can you be so sure? One minute the statues were there, the next they weren't."

Leod laughed. He limped around his desk and took a seat. He brushed the hood from his head, letting it pool around his shoulders. Leod's once-handsome appeal had been marred at the hands of a MacKinnon. He sighed, brushing his fingertips along the misshapen flesh that had been burned. Now he used it to his advantage. It gave him a more frightening appearance when it came to his lesser-minded followers. The disfigurement to the left side of his face and ear startled most, but not this oversized buffoon.

Draven's gaze hardened when Leod met his eyes. Mind tricks didn't work on this one. He'd acknowledged that the first time he attempted to control Draven when they met three months ago. He'd accepted the man for what he was, a hired killer, nothing more. His worth had been proven when he shared his newly acquired lair, this underground compound, with Leod and his small band of misfit-magical-wannabes.

The few stragglers they'd gathered from the lowest bowels of London's alleys had no true potential. But he'd needed followers. Idiots who'd believe anything if they thought they'd gain a buck for their efforts. Draven and his men, on the other hand, were more precise in their needs, their abilities to function as a group of thieves. Leod admired Draven's talent for molding his men and had given him the task of transforming his meager group into a more *productive* task force for him to use against the MacKinnons and eventually the world once the book was in his hands.

He glanced at Roy, his right-hand man. It pained him to see the scars Roy had obtained in their most recent skirmish with a few of the MacKinnon brothers. What should've been the fiery demise of his adversaries trapped in a burning dock house ended with a lucky arrow shot into a boat with a leaky fuel line, which instantly produced a fireball. If it hadn't been for Roy's quick actions, Leod would've suffered more than an injured hip. But it cost Roy some hair, an eyebrow and burns that would take time to heal.

Doc hadn't been so lucky. Not being able to swim, he'd drowned. According to the newspaper article, the authorities discovered the body of a disgraced London doctor floating facedown in the river. It was listed as an apparent suicide. Leod leaned comfortably back in his chair. Doc had been a useful tool. Shame to lose such a dedicated fool.

Looking at Draven, he knew the only thing this man understood was money and power. Both he'd been promised in exchange for his services. Leod grinned inwardly. The joke was on him. Leod had no intentions of sharing the *Book of Shadows*.

"Roy, what time is it?" Leod asked.

Roy retrieved an old watch from his pocket. A thick gold chain attached it to his belt loop. The antique had been Roy's reward for saving him from a fire that broke out at a nightclub. Leod rolled his eyes. That had been another failed confrontation with the MacKinnons. Now it was his time to win. Heat filled his soul and the familiar sizzle of the burn flowed through his veins and itched to escape his fingertips, but he refrained, keeping the heinous desire to destroy something buried for the time being. He'd get his chance to incinerate at least one of the brothers…soon.

"It's seven in the morning, sir," he reported, then returned the watch to his front pants pocket.

"Ahh, the sun has most definitely risen." He grinned directly at Draven. The idiot had gotten his hand broken and had it wrapped in what looked to be a torn bed sheet. A strip of the fabric had been tied into a sling of sorts, which hung around his neck. Too bad Doc was dead. He could've set that for him.

"What the hell has the sun got to do with anything?" Draven practically growled in a demanding tone.

"Everything," Leod replied calmly as he tapped a few keys on his laptop. His grin broadened as he lifted his gaze once again to meet Draven's dark-eyed glare. Slowly he turned the screen to share what he saw. "Take a look at your captive now. Tell me what you see."

Draven's eyes widened and his brow pursed tightly. He grabbed the laptop and lifted it for closer inspection before he looked at Leod. "How the hell did that happen? I don't understand. Where's the man I took hostage?"

Roy snickered as if his question was stupid, and Draven scowled at him. The air thickened between the testosterone junkies, as it usually did. Neither liked the other and even though Leod soothed Roy's angst several times about his placement, Roy still showed no trust toward Draven. It was a point Leod kept tucked in his mental file for future reference for when it came time to dispose of Draven. Roy would gladly handle the deed. Leod interjected before the two came to blows.

"The statue is the man. It seems their release is temporary. It looks as if the twins haven't been given the means with which to break the curse entirely. At least, this one hasn't. Consider this a stroke of luck for us." He grinned widely. "We'll use him as bait to lure the others here. What better way to end Clan MacKinnon than by fire and suffocation."

Draven's eyebrow arched. The deadliest smile Leod had ever seen twisted the man's lips. If he didn't like the look, it surely would've scared a lesser man. "How many are we considering taking out at one time?"

"If my calculations are correct and all the brothers come in search of this missing soul, four plus this one and the other twin if he shows will be a total of six MacKinnons and whoever else might be lost in the explosive cave-in."

"I'm liking those numbers. How do you expect them to find us?"

"Did you not tell me that bumbling idiot Crosby was left behind?" He nodded and Leod continued. "Then I'm quite sure by now he's given the authorities everything they ever wanted to know about me and my operation. Prepare your men for what might be coming our way."

Draven turned for the door but was stopped before he reached it. "Draven." Leod spoke his name in a commanding way that made him look back across his shoulder. "Make sure *all* the MacKinnons gain access to the holding cell's bunker. I don't care what you do to anyone who goes along with them. Is that clear?"

"Loudly," he replied then left, humming a deadly sounding tune.

"How come he gets to have all the fun?" Roy whined.

"Because you, my friend, have another assignment."

Roy's eyes widened with a questioning glare. "What is it you want me to do?"

"Find and kill Kip Crosby. Make sure he's informed them of our location first. Then do what you want with him."

"And Draven?"

"He'll be my present to you when this is done and the MacKinnons are dead."

* * * * *

She woke to the vibration of her phone. Jenny hadn't been in a deep sleep out of fear of someone sneaking up on her. Fifteen-minute catnaps helped her continue to keep watch over Dour without becoming totally exhausted. Her eyes hadn't been closed for long when her phone did a dance on her chest. Lifting the cell so she could see the screen, she couldn't believe it. No signal to make or receive a call but a text message had somehow gotten through.

Keep your cell on and we will find you. Help is on the way.

Jenny sat upright. Who sent this? She climbed from the driver's seat and continued to stare at the message. Should she turn the phone off? What if it was someone from the compound who'd noticed where she was hidden and somehow managed to track her cell signal? She knew the technology was out there. It was possible to locate a person by the GPS device in the phone as long as it remained on. Jenny chewed her lower lip with indecision. Should she or shouldn't she turn it off? Her thumb lingered over the power switch. She couldn't take the chance it came from the compound. Who knew what sort of techno geeks they had employed inside there?

Why would they text her? She stared in the direction of the guardhouse. Wouldn't they take her prisoner if they saw her? That made more sense but still she couldn't be sure of anything, especially the person on the other end of that text.

Just as she was about to press the button, it vibrated. Another text message.

This is the woman from the warehouse. Praying you haven't been taken prisoner. By now you've learned the pitfalls of the anti-curse. Please keep him safe until nightfall or at least until his brothers can get there. Your new friend, May.

Should she trust this May person? Jenny leaned against the car. What to do, what to do? On or off? What if this was a trick perpetrated by someone from the compound to lure her into a false sense of security? She inhaled deeply, trying to quell her nerves. Her eyes widened as she reread the words. Pitfalls of the anti-curse? What anti-curse?

Ancient words resurfaced in her head. The woman had spoken something in front of the crate right before the ground shook and thick dust filled the room. Was that an anti-curse? Jenny stared at the brown blanket covering the upper half of Dour. The lower edge of his kilt to his feet was visible. She turned her attention back to the phone.

Should she try texting back? Her insides churned. Indecision was making her nauseated, or was it simply hunger? Jenny leaned inside the car and dug another protein bar and a second water bottle from the backpack. Maybe if she ate something she'd think clearer. Checking the time on her phone, she saw it was almost noon. How long would it take this so-called help to find her? What would they do when they got there?

Would Cait even be alive when they did?

Her chest tightened. She refused to believe in the negative. She and Cait would both get through this, a bit worse for wear, but alive. This she was determined would happen. Jenny hung the binoculars around her neck. She moved to the front of the car and leaned against the hood as she searched the compound for any signs of her best friend or Dour's brother. Nothing. There was minimal movement above ground with the exception of the two guards at the gate and a series of armed patrols she'd spotted occasionally walking the perimeter of the barbed-wire fence.

That didn't mean something wasn't happening below ground. Jenny's shoulders sagged as she lowered the binoculars. She had no choice but to trust the unknown at the other end of that text. Retrieving the cell phone from her pocket, she responded.

I truly hope I'm not making a mistake & what you said is true. We are located near the border of Scotland. Not sure exactly where. Hiding outside a bunker community, which seems to be armed and guarded.

She said a silent prayer before she hit send.

Taking up watch with the binoculars again, she scoured the area, looking for anything that might help in Cait's rescue. Something caught her eye. As careful as a mouse avoiding a hawk, she moved toward the tree line closest to the compound. Squatted behind the underbrush, she focused on an oddity in the fencing. It appeared as if an animal had burrowed underneath the wire. If she approached it at just the right angle, she could use the only visible building onsite—some sort of storage barn—as cover, blocking the guardhouse's view. She'd have to time it with the patrol's maneuvers.

Lying quietly, she watched and timed their rounds. Her neck ached and she did her best not to let the sun hit the binoculars and give away her position. When she was certain she had their schedule down pat, she eased back into the brush and thick of the trees, returning to Dour and the car.

Her cell phone vibrated again and relief washed over her as she read the words.

We have your location. Keep hidden and the MacKinnon brothers will be there by nightfall when the twins wake.

Keep hidden. That was exactly what she was trying to do. Jenny moved to the front of the car and leaned on the hood. She lifted the blanket from Dour's face. The pain in his eyes made her ache. It must've hurt to have his freedom for such a brief time. Her left eyebrow lifted as that last message poked her curiosity. She dropped the blanket's edge and looked at her phone again. Pulling up the last message, she reread it.

Key words burned in her brain. Nightfall. Wake. Excitement stirred in her gut as a spark of heat ignited and spread, warming her. Dour would wake at nightfall. Did that mean what she thought it meant? He'd be free of the curse again, but for how long?

Jenny rolled the blanket back from his face, bunching it on top of his head. She sat facing him and touched his outstretched hand. Did he know she was there? Did he know he'd be free when the sun went down? Thinking back to the warehouse, she didn't remember the woman saying anything about it then, but events happened so fast. She could've said it and Jenny missed it.

It had to be horrible being trapped. She gently rubbed his hand and prayed he knew he'd be free in a few hours. Jenny pressed her lips to his ear and whispered, "Help is on the way."

She hoped he heard her but she had no way of knowing if he did or didn't. And that help was in the form of MacKinnon brothers. Were they Dour's brothers? Had they also been cursed? Confusion contorted her thoughts. This curse thing was a bit too much to consume at one time.

A heavy rustling in the limbs above her head made her jump. Catching sight of a squirrel, she took a breath and shook her head at her uneasiness. Who wouldn't be scared and on edge in a situation like this? She wrapped her arms around herself as she made a quiet pass around their perimeter, making sure it was truly only a squirrel that startled her.

The need to be near him made her settle on the ground at his feet. She curled into a ball against his legs and prayed he wasn't suffering in his magically induced prison. Questions tumbled through her tired brain.

Could he breathe? Did he need to breathe? Was he alive or in some partially dead sort of condition? A state of suspended animation, so to speak. She nuzzled against him, wanting him as close to her as possible. She needed this connection to feel secure. It was her against a compound full of crazies until the others reached her or Dour woke, whichever came first. Closing her eyes, she prayed the enemy wouldn't find them and that Dour was okay and Cait and Donnell weren't hurt.

Was Donnell a statue too? He had to be. The curse had stricken them both. Jenny hoped Cait understood what was going on, but how could she? Cait had no way of knowing the effects of the curse. She had to be scared shitless. Lord knew what those creeps were doing to them. Jenny closed her eyes tight for a moment, trying to send Cait a wave of strength to see her through this odd adventure. It was only a matter of time before help arrived. She had to keep the faith for all of their safety.

Though she doubted Cait would receive it underground, she sent her a text message. *Help is on the way. Be safe. Stay close to Donnell. When night falls, he will waken.* She prayed heavily the words reached her friend. *If* she was still alive.

Trying to redirect her thoughts from the worst, she shook it from her mind and forced something pleasant to surface. Thinking of Dour's kiss made her smile. She liked the way he kissed her. Even though their sexual escapade in the car hadn't exactly been the picture of perfection, they'd both gotten off. Absently she brushed the tender spot on her head where she'd hit the roof several times, but it was worth it. She had a small bruise on her hip from the gearshift that really didn't matter. She'd do it again in the car if he wanted.

Even better, she wanted to take him home and share the oversized memory foam mattress she'd treated herself to a few months ago. It hadn't been broken in as yet and she couldn't think of anyone else she'd like to test it with other than Dour. Sex with him in that bed would be awesome. The two of them stretched out side by side naked, tasting and touching each other, exploring every nuance of foreplay possible until they were raw and sated. Her nipples tingled at the thought. Just thinking about sex with him had her wet, willing and wanting.

Jenny tightened her arms around her knees, clasping them to her chest. Never had she reacted in such a way to a man. Dour wasn't just a man. He was a hunky Scottish laird from a time long forgotten. It turned her on even more thinking about being in his arms, about teaching him the ways of this era. Her eyebrow arched. Yeah. She definitely wanted to be the one to show him how this world worked. The life he knew no longer existed and someone needed to help him. Why not her?

She did her best to relax even though every little noise, every whistle of the breeze through the trees had her looking for intruders. Her senses were keyed on high alert and her nerves were stretched thin. Jenny caught herself checking the time on her cell phone every few minutes.

This was going to be the longest day of her life.

Chapter Ten

Cait woke to the sense of being watched. For several long seconds, she didn't move on the cot as she got her bearings. On the pretense of washing the tears from her face, she got up and walked over to the sink. She rinsed the washcloth while using the small mirror on the wall to survey the room without being obvious. If she didn't know what she was looking for, she would've missed it. A circular mark high on the wall above the door gave away the camera's location. She finished the face-washing process, tidied the sink and neatly folded the cloth and hung it to dry on the basin's edge.

She wasn't wrong. They were watching them and she had no doubt they knew Donnell's current condition. So what was the next move going to be? She checked her wristwatch. Noon. She'd slept a few hours and it didn't appear as if they'd entered the room while she'd done so. What were they up to? It baffled her. They'd taken them hostage, thrown them in this room and then left them alone. Why? Why not question them? *About what?* She nearly laughed at herself over that one. What did she know? Absolutely nothing. Or at least nothing that was of any worth to this nutcase Brother Leod in her opinion.

From the position of the camera, she bet it followed her every step around the room. If her calculations were right, the only place it couldn't see was directly below it in front of the door.

With this roving eye upon her, escape proved more difficult but not impossible. She turned her back to the door as she smiled. Nothing was impossible as far as she was concerned. Looking at Donnell, she knew she needed a plan. Something that included hauling a man of stone out of this cell because there was no way she was leaving him behind.

Slowly she moved around Donnell, doing her best to mentally guess his weight. She doubted she'd be able to lift him. There was no way she'd carry him out on her back. Determined to see if she could even move him, she gave him a great big hug, doing her best to reach all the way around. It didn't matter if the people watching thought she was nuts hugging an inanimate object, it gave her proof she couldn't lift or even nudge him an inch in this state.

Damn. This was going to be a challenge. She sat on the floor facing him. His distressed expression tore at her heart. Was he in pain? Did he know she was here? She snorted at her ridiculousness. How the hell had she gotten herself into this nightmare? Oh yeah. She'd listened to a drunk and believed his wild tale about a crazy man, a curse and a book of black magic spells.

She sat back on her heels but let her hands linger on his as they lay frozen to his legs in his kneeling position. He'd been about to stand and now he was stuck that way forever. Cait bit her lower lip as an idea brewed. But was he? Something the drunken idiot had told her sizzled in the back of her brain, trying its best to burn its way to the forefront. What had he said? Her eyes widened as the memory surfaced.

Curse of the Gargoyle. That's what he said the curse was called that supposedly this Leod person's ancestor had used on a long-lost clan. What happened to the mythical gargoyle creatures? They turned to stone during the daylight hours and returned to life at night. Cait swallowed her excitement, not wanting the individuals on the other end of that camera to think she'd figured out something important.

But was it?

If it had been some sort of gargoyle curse, then why hadn't he shifted back and forth the entire time? She leaned against the cot but never lowered her eyes from his petrified gaze. Softly spoken ancient words drifted through her head and it hit her. It had to be related to the poem from the redhead at the warehouse. Whatever she'd said set this scheme in motion and broke the twins free. It had to be a mixture of the original curse with this sort of anti-curse. Maybe the anti-curse wasn't whole.

Cait knew she was grasping at straws with this theory but it was all she had to keep her going. Would Donnell come back to life at nightfall just like a gargoyle? She casually glanced at the camera, then returned her gaze to his. Lord, she hoped so. Even captured in a wall of solid stone, he was one hot-damn-good-looking man. She snuggled close and hoped without hope her half-baked idea was right.

Donnell was a gargoyle.

* * * * *

May quickly learned Jameson's bodyguard-chauffeur was more than he seemed. Charles Maxwell was a former Navy SEAL who was injured while on a mission. His talents amazed her. He'd spent the night outside her hotel room door on guard. Jameson told her Charles had gathered intel on everyone involved with the warehouse break-in. He used the video feed from the cameras set up both outside and inside the warehouse to attempt to identify the thieves and paired it with a facial recognition program installed in his computer. Unfortunately, it took time shifting through hundreds of thousands of images.

When the MacKinnons arrived, Ian's computer-whiz fiancée, Izzy, wasted no time helping Charles. The pair avidly worked as a team. May loved having her family around her. It helped ease the knot in her chest and gave her hope they would succeed in bringing the twins home. The waiting as Izzy and Charles tried different avenues weighed on her nerves.

They tracked the owner of the Beetle through the license plate. It belonged to a Cait Milner. By the time he and Izzy were done, they had extensive information on both Cait and her business partner, Jenny Baker. May read the list of information Charles handed her.

The pair met while in college. They shared a flat outside London where they owned and operated an online paranormal magazine. Their bank records showed they struggled financially, barely making ends meet. There were copies of their birth certificates, school transcripts and phone records and proof of no arrests between them. She flipped through and found photos with their names beside them.

Her brows pursed as she questioned Charles. "This is both amazing and scary that you were able to get all of this in a matter of hours."

As he returned to the chair beside Izzy at the desk, Charles stated in a matter-of-fact way, "No information is safe. If someone with the right skills wants to know your life history, it's a matter of clicks on a keyboard."

"Where'd you get these pictures of the ladies from the warehouse?" May asked.

"It wasn't that hard," Izzy replied without looking up from the laptop. "Once Charles helped me break motor vehicle's encryption, the rest was easy. Those are their driver's license photos."

Charles' computer beeped and he let out a low whistle as he read the screen. "This is not good."

"What?" May and Jameson both stated simultaneously.

He spoke as he sent the info to print. "Seems we're dealing with a real bad-ass." He swung his chair toward the printer and picked up the picture. He held it for them to see as he explained. "Meet one of Interpol's most wanted, Clay Draven. He's been linked to several murders, four armored car heists and is suspected of being the ringleader of one of the roughest gangs around."

May dropped onto Jameson's lap. Her heart sank. "Please tell me Leod hasn't teamed with these people." Jameson's arms wrapped around her.

"I can't tell you that for a fact," Charles stated. "Draven's usual marks are big deposits of cash, not art, so it's a possibility he's been hired for this job." His computer beeped again and he printed off another picture. Holding it up, he said, "This one makes more sense than Draven." He flipped it for them to see. "Kip Crosby. Arrested for selling art and artifacts on the black market."

"Did you say Kip Crosby?" Struan's girlfriend, Caledonia, questioned as she moved closer.

"You know him?" Charles asked, handing her the picture.

Nodding, she replied coldly, "He's my ex-husband. How in the hell did he get out of jail? Last I heard, his parents wanted nothing to do with him and he couldn't afford a lawyer."

Charles shrugged. "Someone posted bail, which he jumped. He's been missing for four months."

"Any idea who was behind his release?" May questioned as she touched Caledonia's arm. Kip blamed Caledonia for his ending up in jail. He'd stolen Struan in statue form and tried to sell him to an infamous black market dealer. If Caledonia hadn't arrived when she did, Struan probably wouldn't be with them. May did her best to soothe Cali.

After a few clicks on the computer, Charles had the answer. "Some charity group called The Brotherhood of the Sons of the Servant of Judgment."

"Son of a bitch," Caledonia groaned.

Struan was at her side, consoling her. "Cali, this no be your fault. He chose his path. If it be vengeance he seeks, than he shall face me man to man."

Struan towered over Caledonia and seemed to swallow her in his arms as he comforted her. He led her to the couch where they sat talking quietly between them. May smiled, knowing he'd ease Cali's distress better than anyone else in the room. Struan had been found at the bottom of a lake and freed by Caledonia, a jet-black-haired beauty with the strangest color of blue eyes May had ever seen.

Looking around the room, it warmed her heart to see the good that came from the turmoil of this curse. Her once-introverted niece, Ericka, was now married to the eldest MacKinnon brother, Gavin, and expecting their first child. She was curled in a comfortable chair with her eyes closed, resting. Strands of her auburn hair escaped her bun and outlined her angelic face. May knew she wasn't asleep, not with all this going on. Ericka simply obliged Gavin's wishes to rest for the baby's sake.

Gavin stood, arms crossed, staring out the window as if in deep thought. His dark hair hung between his shoulders tied with a leather strap. All the brothers had similar features, were healthily built, varied in height from six foot and over and believed in the old ways. Ian was engaged to the beautiful, techno-savvy Izzy. He and Padon sat in chairs they'd moved closer to Gavin and were steadily sharpening their swords and knives. These were the weapons of their time and May truly hoped it didn't come down to a battle with this so-called bad-ass group of that Draven person. Chills shot down her spine as she prayed for a peaceful solution.

Padon was the last brother to be released from the curse. He'd been discovered in a cave and brought home by a sweet Texan named Lynn. At the moment, May was thankful for Lynn's patient nature. It was a trait she knew

Lynn needed for the task they'd given her. The most recent addition to their family, Lynn stayed at Castle MacKinnon to keep the only MacKinnon daughter, Akira, company, especially since she was bound to the grounds as a ghost. But that didn't stop Akira from being fiercely protective of her brothers. Death didn't end her love and devotion to her family. May's heart warmed when she thought of Akira. The bright-redheaded, green-eyed specter had entered her life several years prior and given her a quest—find the MacKinnon brothers and break the curse.

May had gladly accepted. She might not have ever been able to have children of her own, but this family was hers and she'd be damned if she'd let anyone harm them.

It seemed like an eternity passed while Izzy and Charles worked frantically on locating a GPS signal from either of the ladies' cell phones. They weren't able to locate Cait's phone, but they got a hit on Jenny. The signal wasn't easy to locate but they managed to obtain the coordinates from Jenny's phone. Once locked in on her GPS it was a matter of time before they reached her.

Though she hadn't wanted to, May remained behind in the hotel room with Ericka, Izzy and Caledonia. The women and

Jameson were to man the base while the others went to retrieve the twins and the two women with them. The men were headed for the heliport. Charles would fly the helicopter so as not to involve the regular pilot should things get iffy. He planned to stay with the helicopter and be on the ready when they needed to be evacuated once they released the prisoners. He'd made sure Ian knew how to handle the quick-release lock kit he gave him, and Gavin had the ear bud technology down pat before they left the hotel.

Gavin's face at using the device the first time as they practiced was priceless. It had brought a moment of laughter to the tense situation. It should give her some relief in her anxiety knowing they were going into this sort of prepared, but it didn't. With Leod, anything was possible. No one knew what devilish tricks he'd have waiting for them.

May twisted her hands as she paced around the table where Izzy sat tapping on a keyboard with an expensive headset covering her ears and an attached mic at her mouth. Izzy was in close contact with the men, who were at the moment in Jameson's personal helicopter heading toward the border. Charles had called in a couple of favors and Izzy was connected to a satellite zoning in on the coordinates of the woman's cell phone. They had a limited window of use but they were hoping to get a visual layout of the compound before the satellite had to be rerouted to its original position.

The favor paid off. After about a minute, Izzy was able to see images of the main compound and saved them to her computer. With the precision of an eagle's eye, she spotted a grove of trees where the woman and one of the twins were possibly hiding. She managed to hold the visual for a few seconds before their window of opportunity closed but it was enough to give them sufficient information about the area.

"Sending you the visual now," Izzy stated.

May peered over Izzy's shoulder at the screen. To her it looked like a bunch of blips and shades of gray, black and white. Jameson's hand touched her elbow. When she met his concerned gaze, he said in a reassuring tone, "Everything is going to be fine."

"I hope you're right," she replied on a heavy sigh.

Chapter Eleven

Throughout the day, Jenny kept watch on the compound with the binoculars. She jotted notes on everything she saw from a truck's arrival and disappearance into the barn to the changing of the guards to a car leaving. There seemed to be minimal action above ground. What happened below, she had no idea. Occasionally a door into a bunker would open and someone would come out or go in. The bunker where she'd seen them take Cait didn't appear as if anyone came or went. They could've moved them while she napped. God, she wished she hadn't done that. Now she couldn't be sure if they were still in there.

As the sun slowly lowered, her anticipation rose. If the woman named May was to be believed, she would no longer be alone. Jenny removed the blanket from Dour. She sat on the hood of the car. Her eyes were glued to the statue, waiting for a miracle. The second the sky streaked with the last rays of sunlight and the golden ball fell behind the horizon, heat filled the air and coated her skin. The statue shook and cracked. A sizzle rippled on the wind and slithered down her spine. Her eyes widened with excitement—she didn't want to miss one moment. Dust and dirt clouded her vision but when it cleared, Dour stood bewildered before her.

Before he got his bearings, she lunged from the hood and nearly toppled him to the ground. Wrapping her arms around his waist she hugged him tight, nuzzling her face against his chest.

"It's you. It's really you."

"Aye," he replied with a hint of humor in his tone. "Who else shall I be?"

His strong hands holding her against him made the stress of her day disappear. She could stay here all night. But she had to save Cait. Jenny leaned back and met his mischievous gaze. "What?" she asked.

"I thought of ye whilst the curse controlled me. It kept me sane."

"You were awake inside the statue?" It amazed her he was calm. She would've been frantic being imprisoned. He claimed he thought of her and it helped him. "You thought of me?"

"Aye." Dour leaned and captured her lips in a passionate kiss. He crushed her to him as if he were afraid to let go, afraid she'd disappear. He broke from their kiss and lifted her hair to his nose. "Mmm, *mi milis subh-làir*—sweet strawberry."

Jenny jumped at the sound of a twig or stick snapping. Dour moved with precision, placing her behind him as he poised, readying for a fight.

"It nay be my intention to intrude," a large man stated, stepping out of the thick brush to stand beside the car. "Now be not the time for romance."

"*Brathair!*" Dour's excitement sounded in his tone. He closed the distance and took the man into a hug. "It gladdens my heart to see ye."

"I wonder if'n he feels the same about us," another male said as three more appeared out of the brush.

"Aye," Dour claimed, taking each in a hug. "It be good to see ye all. How can this be? Were ye cursed as well?"

From the looks of them, they could be brothers. Jenny stood back staring, reaping in the benefit of such a good-looking collection of men. Each was well built, tall and similar in facial features. Two had jet-black hair, one had hair so deeply auburn it was almost black and the other had dark hair with red highlights. Even with the differences in hair colors, they still looked alike. She found it interesting they wore matching kilts. The same as Dour's. Except they also had on dark shirts and black boots with a series of buckles all the way to just below the knee. Dour was barefoot and bare-chested.

"All the men of Clan MacKinnon fell to the curse," Gavin answered.

"Akira?" Dour questioned.

"She still be around to torment us, but not in the way ye remember," one of his brothers replied, then a big smile brightened his face.

"What do ye mean, Ian?" In the dusky light of early evening, Jenny read the confusion in Dour's expression.

"Akira be a ghost. She swore loyalty to protecting us and the angels granted her wish to stay, only she can't leave MacKinnon lands," another brother explained. He turned to Jenny and grinned, then extended his hand. "And who shall this lovely lady be?"

He took her hand and brushed a quick kiss to her knuckles, which was the wrong thing to do apparently. Dour was at her side instantly, taking a protective stance.

"Struan, this be Jenny. She has aided me in my pursuit of Donnell," he stated tersely and Jenny sensed he was jealous his brother had touched her. It made her giddy to think Dour had feelings for her. Or was it simply sibling rivalry?

Refusing to believe the latter, she smiled then replied, "It's nice to meet you, Struan. And who are the others?" She looked at Dour for his answer.

"These are *mi brathairs*, Gavin, Ian and Padon," he announced. Each nodded as he introduced them. Dour looked around then back to Gavin. "Where be Aiden?"

Gavin's expression darkened, as did that of all the other brothers as he informed sadly, "He has not been found as yet."

Jenny touched Dour's arm. She hated to interrupt the family reunion but her best friend was being held captive and was probably dead for all she knew. "With reinforcements here, what are we going to do about your brother and my best friend? They've got guns. What do we have?"

The one named Ian lifted a crossbow and grinned. "It no be my practice to miss what I aim at with this."

Her eyebrow arched as each brother produced a weapon. Swords, knives and a crossbow. Would they be a match against guns? "Let's hope it doesn't come to that. Maybe we can sneak in and out before anyone is the wiser."

As she spoke the words, doubt planted a seed in her heart and another question fired from her lips. "How did y'all get here? I didn't hear anything drive close to us."

Ian responded as he repositioned his crossbow. "We arrived by flight, milady."

This confused her even more. "I didn't hear—"

Gavin interrupted her with a quick explanation. "We have a friend waiting in a helicopter about a mile from here. He dropped us as close as possible without being spotted. We hiked the rest of the way. He awaits our word to pick us up." He touched his ear and it was the first time she noticed a tiny device positioned inside. Damn. She didn't get the chance to ask or think.

"We sat hidden in the trees across the field until nightfall. Now we're here and there's much to be done," Gavin spoke as he moved to the hood of the car, pulled a small computer tablet from a pouch hung low on his hip and motioned for everyone to gather around. Looking at the ancient man, she was impressed. He must've read her surprised look as he stared directly at her. "I was freed from the curse first. My wife has great patience with me and has taught me much in the ways of today's world. With luck, ye shall meet her upon our return."

Jenny simply nodded and he continued. "We need a plan of attack. This is an image of the compound. Do you know which of these bunkers contains the hostages?"

"Wow. How did you get this? It's definitely not a Google Earth thing." She met his gaze. A sly smile tickled his lips for a second but disappeared, replaced by an emotionless, stoic expression. One she guessed was his battle face.

"Let's just say we have friends with amazing powers."

She started to ask but swallowed her questions. Jenny retrieved her notes from the front seat of the car and moved to stand beside him. After a moment, she pointed on the tablet's screen to the last place she'd seen Cait. "I saw them being forced into that one. But I can't be sure they are still there. I wasn't able to stay awake the whole time. They could've been moved during one of my naps. I did manage to locate a place of possible entry and I noted the shift changes of the guards and how often they pace the compound."

Gavin nodded. "Good work. This will come in handy. It be doubtful they moved them. It would present an opportunity for escape."

Jenny wanted to believe he was right even though she figured he was saying what he thought she needed to hear to make her feel better. She showed them on the screen where she'd seen the gap in the fencing and its location in relation to the barn. "I think an animal may have dug underneath. I saw a van go in there earlier but never saw it leave. It's quite possible it's a location to house their supplies."

"Okay," Gavin said as he studied the screen along with her detailed account of their actions throughout the day. "This just might work." He laid out their plan, leaving no possibility unturned. He checked what looked like to her to be an extremely old pocket watch he pulled from his pouch. "We've got exactly fifty-two minutes before the guards make another pass around this side." He tucked the tablet in his pouch, along with Jenny's notes.

Ian removed one of two straps that lay across his chest from shoulder to hip and handed it to Dour. "Ye might be in need of this, *mi brathair*."

Dour's face lit up as he took hold of it and slid it easily from its sheath. "My sword. How? Where?"

Ian laughed as he slapped Dour on the back. "Ye can thank Akira for that one. She hid our weapons and prize possessions in Gavin's tower and haunted it to protect it. No soul ever made it past her watchful eye."

She wasn't sure how it was possible, but Dour's smile broadened more. "That sounds like her." He did a practice maneuver with the claymore before returning it to its sheath and situating it comfortably on his back. After he reached over his shoulder and relieved the sword of the sheath easily, he was satisfied with its location. He sighed. "My soul be whole again."

Looking around, she noticed each brother had a sword that seemed antique in quality except for Ian. "What happened to your sword? Did your sister not like you and let someone take yours? Is that why you carry a crossbow?"

He grinned, lifting his weapon. "I prefer the bow and arrow to the steel. Milady Izzy gifted me with this latest adaptation of the crossbow, and I have to say," he winked at her, "I like it. It be quite powerful and the shorter arrows are accurate." He wore a quiver of arrows strapped to his hip.

"If everyone is ready, let's get into position." Gavin looked from one brother to the other as each gave him the okay nod. "May the Gods be with us."

When Jenny moved to go with them, Gavin halted her. "Ye be safer here. Remain near the car and be ready to go the moment we return." He dug in his pouch and produced another ear bud. "We shall be needing eyes at our back. That be your job."

"But—" A hand on Jenny's shoulder stopped her from continuing.

She turned to face Dour. His eyes were dark and his face showed concern. His hand cupped her chin. "I would never forgive myself if'n ye were hurt during this battle. Please remain here. Ye have been brave enough for one day. Ye protected me whilst I slept. Be assured we shall free your friend Cait and *mi brathair* Donnell and return unscathed."

The confidence in his words warmed her, but it was the way he sealed it with a kiss loaded with promise that touched her heart and convinced her to listen.

Chapter Twelve

Heat warmed her skin and a sort of electrical current sizzled around her. Cait sat upright on the cot, facing Donnell. The statue vibrated, dust thickened the air and she couldn't help but smile. A glance at her wristwatch and she knew she was right. The gargoyle was awakening. The only thing she hated about this moment was the camera on the wall. Their captors watched this happen and possibly recorded it. That thought made her cringe. This was definitely something they didn't want to end up on the Internet. At the moment there wasn't anything she could do about it.

She blinked, clearing her vision. Her heart skipped a beat at the sight of Donnell alive and breathing once again. She stood, uncertain as to what she should say or do. Her insides twisted into a ball of nerves as the moment lasted for what seemed like an eternity until he reached for her. His embrace squeezed away any indecision and made her respond by hugging him in return. This was nice. She had to admit his strong arms wrapped around her gave her a moment of peace in an otherwise stressful day of unrest. Cait hadn't been sure if her gargoyle theory was correct and spent hours trying to deduce a plan of escape and a way to take Donnell's statue with her.

Now she didn't have to worry. He was free to help them get out of there. A trickle of moisture ran down Cait's cheek and she leaned back, touching her face. Red appeared on her fingertips. Looking up, she noted the cut under his eye had reopened.

"Donnell, you're bleeding again."

"'Tis nothing a kiss from milady wouldn't fix." He leaned as if to kiss her but she halted him by pressing her fingers to his lips and grabbing him by the elbow.

"You need to sit so I can reach that cut before you bleed to death."

After making him sit on the cot, she carefully extracted the kit from her back pocket, keeping it hidden from the camera as she walked to the sink. She rinsed the cloth and used it to hide the kit. The items in it were the only tools they had to aid in their escape and she wasn't about to lose it by letting them see it. With her back to the camera, she opened the zipper and eased out the foil packet of antibiotic gel.

Cait positioned herself facing Donnell. He spread his legs, giving her room to stand between them. "Here be where I like ye," he stated as he grabbed her by the hips and tugged her forward.

Shaking her head, she couldn't help but grin. "You're impossible. Is sex all you think about? We really need to be figuring out a way to escape," she replied in a whispered tone, hoping they didn't hear them.

One hand caressed her bottom, making it difficult to concentrate on tending his eye, while the other lifted his kilt, showing he stood rigid at attention. Looking at it made her tingle, wanting another go with the sexy Scottish laird. It was all she could do not to touch it.

"With ye, milady, sex be all I can think about. The vision of your beauty filled my mind whilst in captivity. All I kept thinking of were your bountiful breasts, fine arse, tasty lips and sensual eyes. It be no wonder I woke ready to please ye."

His eyes darkened with passion and she nearly melted. Her fingers trembled as she tenderly stroked him but froze when she remembered the camera. She jerked her hand away. Her stomach churned. They'd had sex earlier and she didn't doubt for a second they were watched—closely.

"As much as I'd like to," Cait stated softly, "we're being watched. I'd rather keep our adventures private if you don't mind."

He looked around the room as he spoke. "I no understand. I see no windows."

She cupped his chin and stared directly in his eyes. She kept her voice low as she explained. "There is something called a camera above the door. It acts as a portal into here so people on the outside can see in without windows. Don't look at it. I don't want them to know we know about it. Now hold still so I can take care of your eye."

Regretfully, Cait removed his hand from her arse and turned it palm up between them. "Here, hold this and be helpful instead of a distraction." She laid the kit open in his hand so she could access it easily without being seen.

The stern look in his eyes let her know he didn't like being watched as he followed her lead and kept his voice quiet. "I no understand this camera."

Cait cleaned his cut and kept pressure on it until the bleeding stopped, then applied antibiotic to the wound. "There are a lot of things about this world you don't know. When we get out of here, I'll be happy to teach you."

His eyebrow arched and a mischievous gleam appeared in his eyes. "I promise to be a proper student if'n ye reward me with," he replied huskily, "your body."

Heat ignited deep within her. It amazed her how easily the man turned her on with simply the words he'd spoken. "You want my body as your reward to learn?" she questioned.

"Aye." He nodded. "Thinking of you was the only thing that made my prison tolerable."

"You thought of me? You were awake inside the stone?" Her heart pounded as his words from earlier sank in as well. He'd envisioned her breasts, her arse and her eyes and it kept him sane. This was awful. He was trapped and all he could do was think. "Could you move? Could you breathe?"

He shook his head. "Nay. I could not move and I did not need to breathe for some odd reason. It has to be the magic of the curse. Only my mind functioned." He ran his free hand up the back of her thigh to caress her bottom. "Ye were my savior, *mi brèagha neamhnaid*. I did not know what happened or why or if I would be free again. I sought solace in your beauty and was grateful for the night I had with ye. If it was my final memory, then it was a wonderful one to last me for eternity."

A lump formed in her throat and her heart expanded. No one had ever said such to her. She'd be a memory to last forever.

His hand slid from her rear up her back, slowly slipped around to brush between her breasts, then caught her by the nape of the neck and tugged her forward. "I need to taste your lips. If'n ye grant me this, I shall behave until we escape. I promise."

There was no denying him this one little pleasure, especially after what he'd just admitted. She wanted this kiss as well. Cait leaned in. Lip to lip they touched softly, tasting each other, gently nipping the tender flesh before unleashing the barely controlled passion, deepening the connection. If it were up to her, they'd stay lip-locked until they fucked each other into oblivion. But there were eyes upon them and here was not the place nor the time.

Regretfully she pulled from the kiss and struggled to take a full breath. This man was one of a kind with a sexual aura she was weak to resist, but she had no choice. They had to get out of here and soon. Carefully she returned the remainder of the antibiotic to the kit and zipped it. Instead of tucking it in her back pocket, since it faced the camera, she slipped it into her bra and shifted her breasts to conceal it.

Donnell's eyebrow hitched and a devious look appeared. "Ye are a tease, milady. It no be fair ye get to touch the very part of ye I hunger to play with and suckle."

Cait shook her head. "You really are incorrigible." He frowned so she leaned, pressing her forehead to his as she whispered, "But I like it. If we were anywhere else, you wouldn't be lacking a riding partner right about now."

He cupped her chin and held her face in place, gaze-to-gaze. "Then let us find a way out of here. My shaft wishes nothing more than to feel the heat of your sheath wrapped around it." He pressed a quick kiss to her lips, then released her.

"Ye have any notions on how we are to escape?" he asked quietly.

His hands rested casually on her hips as if that were the most natural place for them to be. Cait had to admit, she liked his hands upon her but it made it difficult to think straight. She took a breath, determined to focus on the issue of most importance. Escape. Then she'd fuck him 'til his eyes crossed.

Keeping her voice low, she responded, "No. I find it odd no one has come to take us for questioning. You'd think they'd want to know what we know."

"About what?"

"I don't know." She shrugged, as she remained standing between his thighs with her back to the camera. It tore at her concentration knowing he was wanting and ready for her, but being an exhibitionist wasn't her style. "I'm not even sure why they took us."

"They took us because of me."

"You? Why?" For a second, Cait was more confused than ever, until she thought it through. What did this have to do with Donnell? True, they'd tried to steal him from the warehouse when he was in statue form, so this really could be about him.

"I am not sure as to the why," Donnell replied. "The reason behind being cursed eludes me. One minute *mi brathair* and I were asleep, the next it's hundreds of years later. I have no answers for ye but we are locked in here because of me. I don't plan to be locked in here much longer. Does that little pouch of yours contain any sort of weapon?"

"There's a small pocketknife." When she started to slip her hand inside her shirt, he caught her wrist.

"If'n anyone be searching your luscious bounty for treasure, it be me." He released her, then gently slid his hand under her shirt and went straight for her bra. Every brush of his fingers to her flesh sent chills down her to stir trouble in her mound. As if she needed to be primed for action. She'd wanted him since the moment he woke, and now with his hand inside her bra, caressing her nipple, the need intensified and almost fried her brain. She grabbed his arm.

"That's not the kit." She gave him as stern a look as she could muster with her thought pattern stuck on sex.

He grinned. "My mistake." He released her nipple. He managed to cup her breast, caressing it as he carefully removed the kit, keeping it hidden from the camera.

Cait cleared her throat as she undid the zipper and laid it open in his large hand. Whispering, she explained the items. Like a typical man, mischievous excitement shone in his eyes when she touched the firecracker and told him what it did.

"Here's the pocketknife." She pulled it out and showed him how it worked. It had a slender blade a couple inches long, a corkscrew, a screwdriver and a spoon. He palmed it, keeping it out of sight, then tucked it into his kilt.

She realized the flashlight was missing, then checked her front pants pocket. It was there. A quick touch of the switch let her know the battery still had some life, so she replaced it in its spot in the kit. For some reason, she removed the firecracker and matches, then tucked them in her pocket for easier access. She wasn't sure what she planned to do with them but had a feeling they might come in handy. As an afterthought she grabbed the hand sanitizer out of the kit as well and put it in her other pocket. Once done, she replaced the kit in her bra and had to swallow the laugh at the look of disappointment on Donnell's face.

"I promise," she leaned close and reassured him, "as soon as we are out of here and safe, my breasts become your playground."

His face brightened. "I hope that means what I think it means."

"It does."

He cleared his throat. "Then let us take our leave. Ye say they have not been in since they brought us here."

"No."

Donnell held her waist, guiding her backward as he stood. "Then it be time that they do."

He walked to the door and pounded on it. When there was no response, he pounded again and yelled, "Anyone out there?"

This time he got an answer in the form of a male voice shouting, "Hold it down in there."

He pounded harder then replied, "We no be holding it down, as ye say, until ye feed the lass. She be faint."

Cait pressed her ear to the door but heard only muffled voices. She couldn't make out what they said until the same guy yelled back. "I'll see what I can do. Just keep it down in there."

She looked at Donnell and whispered, "Now what?"

He grinned and got close to her ear as he answered, "We wait, then ye shall follow my lead."

* * * * *

Waking had been a relief to his soul. Doubt and fear had clouded his mind on and off throughout his imprisonment. If it had not been for him concentrating on the beautiful Jenny, he might have given up hope on the possibility his entombment was temporary. That sliver of insecurity, of not knowing, nearly sent him mentally over the edge but

Jenny was the rope that bound him. She'd been his salvation and he'd left her behind.

Dour hated leaving Jenny but had no choice. Where they were headed was not safer than where she was hidden. Gavin gave her specific instructions to make the car ready to leave at a moment's notice and she'd agreed. He'd given her an odd-looking item she'd placed in her ear. Apparently it kept her in contact with them. She was to keep watch with the binoculars and warn of any changes as they tried to enter the compound unnoticed. She was their lookout. Knowing she had his back gave Dour a sort of inner peace. She wouldn't let anything happen if she could help it.

He forced his focus on following his *brathairs*. They were heading into battle to free his twin. In his heart, he knew Donnell was alive, thus Jenny's friend Cait had to be as well. It impressed him how Gavin handled the oddities of this time. A thing that glowed and gave Gavin a map of the area made no sense to Dour. Something in Gavin's ear kept him in contact with Jenny and someone named Charles, who apparently was standing by to fly in and pick them up. Fly in? He really didn't want to try to think about that one. Since when did a man fly and how was he going to pick them up?

Gavin showed no confusion over it. Nor did any of his *brathairs*. How long had they been released that they accepted and understood these strange things? In the past Gavin led and they followed his orders without question. He was the head of their clan. Now in this new era things were different. Were families still considered to be clans?

Questions he'd not thought to ask speared his brain. Did his *brathairs* suffer the same as he? When the sun rose would they turn to stone, become a family of solid-rock statues? Did they too suffer this temporary relief, man by night and stone by day? Was this a repetitive sequence? He didn't know. Would he shift again in the light of day? If so, how many years were the MacKinnon *brathairs* deemed to live this harsh cycle?

Most importantly, was there a way to defeat this curse? To be completely free? *Och,* he wished there had been time for such a talk. Dour breathed in deeply, trying to squelch the tumble of thoughts, ideas and questions. Now was not the time for talk. Now was the time for action and he had better remain focused on the battle. Donnell needed him and he would not fail. He logged those questions away until later and fell into step, bringing up the rear.

Silently they crept through the underbrush and trees until they reached the area where the animal had dug under the fence. Gavin crawled toward it while the others hung back in hiding. It took him a matter of seconds to cut an opening large enough in the fence for them to clear. Once he was on the other side and had taken a post to protect them, he gave them the signal to advance.

Not a moment was wasted as they scurried through the fence and took their positions. Dour tripped over a body, caught himself from falling, then looked to Ian, who whispered, "Had no choice. He came around the barn."

"Is he dead?" Gavin asked.

"No," Ian replied. "Unconscious."

Without a word, Struan whipped a piece of twine out of the pouch on his hip and hog-tied the unconscious man and then stuffed a wad of cloth in his mouth. He and Ian dragged him into the shadows of the barn and left him where he wouldn't be easily found. Struan stated softly, "He won't be causing a problem when he wakes."

Gavin took point. Carefully, they maneuvered their way across the compound to the bunker where Jenny had seen the prisoners taken. It took a few moments to find the door, since it blended well with the camouflaged exterior of the bunker. While the others remained vigilantly on watch, Ian worked to open it with tools unfamiliar to Dour. He inserted the tip of a tubular item filled with a clear liquid into the lock. After emptying the contents in it, a puff of smoke appeared as it sizzled and the lock popped, releasing the door.

Dour had no chance to ask questions. A noise came from one of the other bunkers. Gavin, Struan, Padon and Dour drew their swords. With his back against the door, Ian readied his crossbow, aimed in the direction of the sound.

Two men stepped out of the door from the closest bunker to them. The group melded into the shadows, watching and waiting to be discovered. Dour held his breath, hoping for the best but expecting the worst. If it came to it, he and his *brathairs* would not hesitate to kill in self-defense. His family was not cowards. They were known to defend what was rightfully theirs.

From the direction the men were headed, he guessed it must've been changing of the guards at the front gate. He didn't take a full breath until the men were across the compound. That meant they had a matter of about thirty minutes before the patrol made another pass through the area where they'd entered the fence. Even though Padon had pushed the fence together to conceal the damage, it would fail any close inspection and quite possibly give them away.

Dour didn't like this strict time constraint. It added tension to the situation. Ian succeeded in unlocking the door. One by one they slipped in. Once inside, Gavin made a motion and Dour knew Jenny must've spoken to him through the ear thingy. He confirmed Jenny informed him about activity at the gate. The tunnel was dimly lit and descended into the ground. The farther they walked, the cooler the temperature. At the end, they came to another locked door.

Gavin whispered, "Follow my lead."

He boldly tapped on the door, which surprised Dour. It made more sense than wasting time with Ian and his tools. Gavin leaned into the door with the intent of adding enough force to knock whoever was on the other side to the ground. Everyone made ready for whatever stood waiting for them.

The lock clicked.

The door swung open rapidly, throwing their plan off balance. Gavin lunged forward, was grabbed and thrown several feet. He tucked and rolled, then sprang upright into a fighting stance. Ian ran in, ready for the fight, but was quickly stopped short by someone snatching him by the arm and spinning him into a headlock. A sharp but rather tiny knife pressed to his neck. Struan followed, caught a full face of something sprayed by a hand sticking out from behind the door and stumbled about blindly. Padon hit the door, crushing whoever was attached to the spray. The hand dropped the bottle.

Dour entered with his sword drawn, ready to fight, but swallowed his laughter at the sight that met his eyes. Relief washed over him.

"It shall take more than that to pierce my thick skin," Ian pronounced loudly. The man suddenly released him, helping him to regain his balance.

"Ian." Donnell grabbed him in a hug. "Am I ever so glad to see ye."

"As am I," Ian claimed, returning the hug to the man who moments ago tried to skewer him with nothing more than a child's toy. The other brothers followed suit, each expressed their happiness to see him, especially Dour.

"Did ye suffer the curse again?" Dour asked clasping his *brathair* tight in a brotherly bear hug.

"Aye," Donnell replied as he leaned back looking Dour in the eye. "Did ye?"

Dour nodded. His brows pursed as he looked around. "Where be the lass named Cait?"

She stepped from behind the door. Apparently she'd been the reason the door opened so quickly and was the hand behind the hand sanitizing spray that temporarily blinded Struan.

"We've got a problem," Gavin interrupted as he dropped his hand from his ear. "Our eyes on top states the compound sprang to life."

"Jenny," Cait asked, touching his arm. "Is she all right?"

"She be well, milady," he answered. He moved to stand in the circle of brothers. "The lights be on throughout the compound and about fifty people spilled from several bunkers. A group of them have surrounded the door we entered. Seems they expected our arrival. We be trapped. This could get bloody."

Each brother wielded his sword. Ian readied his crossbow. Padon removed the second sheath he carried and handed Donnell his claymore. "Ye be needing this."

With a nod, Donnell replied, "Aye."

Chapter Thirteen

Jenny's heart raced. Her mouth dried. This was bad. This was really, really bad. She forced her hands to steady as she remained focused on the activities of the men at the bunker's door. Their actions had been stalled temporarily by a skirmish that ended with an elderly man being shot. He desperately tried to stop whatever they were doing at the door. On reflex, she'd ducked down beside the car even though they couldn't see her. Her stomach churned and for a few seconds she thought she was going to heave. She'd never seen anyone get shot before, not in real life, only in the movies.

Taking a deep breath to quell her nerves, she returned to her position leaning on the hood with the binoculars glued on the bunker. A small group tried to assist the injured person but was not allowed. If she was reading the situation correctly, it appeared to be some sort of mutiny among the troops. Something definitely wasn't right. A man wearing a monk's robe appeared. Fireballs shot from his hands and the group huddled together. How did he do that? It had to be some sort of magic trick.

Two men with what looked like machine guns surrounded the scared individuals. The monk turned to the large man with a handgun and his arm in a sling. It didn't appear as if he was happy with the man. His next actions had her grinding her teeth. The monk heartlessly stepped over the gunshot victim as if he were nothing more than a speed bump in the road. He wasn't moving and she said a silent prayer for his soul.

She returned her sights to the bunker and her heart stuttered. Several people rolled keg-sized barrels marked *Black Powder* into the tunnel. How the hell did they have that much of something like that? Then it hit her. This used to be a mining area. It quite possibly could've been left behind, forgotten. The barrels looked old and wooden. Her attention shifted to the man who worked outside the door. What was he putting around the door? Jenny didn't know anything about explosives but she'd watched a lot of action movies and this looked like some sort of putty or molding clay. She racked her brain.

C4!

They were lining the exit and loading the tunnel with explosives. Everyone in the bunker would be buried. Her chest pounded and her throat tightened as she sank to the ground beside the car. She had to calm down and relay what she'd seen. Her fingers shook as she pressed the ear bud. In a panic, she told Gavin what she thought was happening on this end and hoped she'd spoken clearly enough.

She shifted onto her knees, leaning against the car, her eyes glued to the binoculars, watching the enemy ants as they scrambled. She'd warned the MacKinnons. Did they have enough time to escape? Could they make it out the same way they went in? Was there another way out?

What could she do to stop this from happening? An idea blossomed. She stood and hurried to the driver's side, slid inside and started the car. She'd drive into the compound, break down the gate if she had to and act like a madwoman. That's what she'd do. She'd make a big scene and stall the impending explosion. Jenny shifted into reverse and twisted to see behind her.

A huge boom echoed and melded her to the seat. A low rumble shook the ground. Her foot slipped off the clutch. The engine stalled. As if the world switched into a slow-motion spin, she turned around and focused on the compound. The trees rustled in the wave of manmade wind. The car vibrated for a split second as if a miniature earthquake happened.

Ohmygod! They'd set it off.

Cait? Dour? The others?

"Gavin," she screamed, pressing the ear bud. No reply came from the group beneath the ground. Only Charles' voice cut the deafening silence.

"What the hell happened?"

"An explosion. Call for help."

Jenny gathered every ounce of strength possible, opened the car door and stood. With heavy hands, she held the binoculars to her eyes but she didn't need them to see the cloud of smoke and dust funneling around the compound. Dirt thickly curtained the area, making it difficult to see even with the bright spotlights. Unfortunately it gave an eerily macabre hue to the whole scene, like a horribly foggy night in London during the reign of Jack the Ripper's terror. Lowering the binoculars, she squeezed her eyes shut, hoping without hope she'd open them and the bad dream would disappear.

It took everything she had to pry her eyelids apart. She dried the tears that fell and looked again. She had to know if there was even a chance of any survivors. The heavy cloud of dust and debris lingered but she couldn't miss the headlights of several vehicles leaving the compound. In her gut she knew one of those carried that demonic monk. She'd never prayed in her life for the demise of another but she did in that moment wish for his death to be extremely painful.

Jenny noted the direction they drove, then returned her attention to the compound. She needed to determine the extent of the damage so she could relay it to the authorities and hopefully get help here immediately. As the dust slowly cleared, her heart sank.

Part of the bunker was gone. What hadn't been scattered across the compound fell into what must've been a tunnel leading underground. In slow motion, sections of the bunker crumbled, adding layer upon layer of dirt into the sunken section. Hope evaded her. Jenny couldn't take any more. Quickly she relayed what she saw to Charles, who told her to stay put until he reached her.

Tears flowed freely as she settled with her back against the wheel well, dragged her knees to her chest and cried. She battled her grief long enough to dig out her cell phone and text.

Please send help. There's been an explosion. A bunker caved in with all the brothers and Cait inside. Communication with them has been lost. Possible multiple casualties. Please help.

* * * * *

May reread the text. It couldn't be. This wasn't happening. She looked at her niece, Ericka. She couldn't tell her Gavin might not be coming back. When she looked from face to face of the women who loved the MacKinnon brothers, reality slapped her hard. There was a possibility none of them would return. A strong hand reached for the wrist of the hand holding the cell phone. She met Jameson's questioning gaze. It took everything she had to speak.

"There's been an explosion. We need to send emergency help immediately." It was all she could say on a whisper before she handed the phone to Jameson.

He quickly took action. She vaguely heard him relaying the coordinates and explaining the situation to someone on the other end. This was not happening. Brother Leod was not winning this battle. Or had he? Her gut twisted into a bundle of electrified nerves.

She gathered the ladies and made them sit upon the couch. Knowing Ericka's delicate condition, she didn't want her to faint and injure herself or the baby by hitting the floor. It damn near killed her to have to tell them the news. She knew she couldn't keep it from them. Ericka, Izzy and Caledonia each stared at her with apprehension on their faces. It was as if they already expected the worst and she was about to confirm it.

May dug deep and managed to make the words exit her lips. "There's been a terrible accident. An explosion. The bunker the brothers went in to rescue Donnell and the young lady from has been destroyed."

Ericka grabbed her stomach. "The men? Gavin?" Panic filled her voice and terror showed in her expression.

"At this point, we don't know."

Ericka turned to Izzy. "Did you hear anything? You were in contact with them, weren't you?"

Izzy shook her head violently as she jumped up and ran to the desk where her laptop sat. "No. I lost contact after they went below ground. Charles warned me that might happen due to distance." She frantically tapped the keys.

Caledonia gathered one of Ericka's hands and calmly stated, "It's going to be all right. Our men are strong. Considering what they've endured, this won't be what kills them." She lifted her gaze to May's. "I believe this, as should we all."

Jameson rolled into the room. "I contacted Charles on his cell phone. He heard the explosion from his position, has been in touch with Jenny and is already in the air searching for them. The explosion didn't go unnoticed. Emergency crews were already en route when I called. Apparently everyone within twenty miles of the event notified the authorities. With all the activity going on there now, I doubt the helicopter will be noticed like it might have been earlier."

Izzy shut her laptop. Caledonia stood and helped Ericka to her feet. The ladies faced May as a united front until pain riddled Ericka's features. Water pooled at her feet. Caledonia wrapped an arm around her waist as May grabbed her hands and helped her return to the couch.

"Looks like we're going to the hospital," May stated. She gave a weak smile. Happiness over the impending birth was overshadowed by the uncertainty of the men's safety.

She turned to ask Jameson to call but he was already on the phone. He clicked it shut and smiled. "The ambulance is on the way."

* * * * *

Due to the baby being a few weeks earlier than expected, a doctor had been assigned to Ericka's care. At first Ericka balked. She wanted Mary Small, the midwife she'd been seeing in Scotland, to deliver the baby. Doctor

Carson agreed that if Ms. Small arrived in time, he'd have no issue with her being present if it made the mother more at ease. May called her. Lucky for them, she happened to be in Edinburgh visiting a relative and not doing her usual rounds in the highlands. This put her much closer to them. Jameson arranged for a private rental helicopter to pick her up. A few hours later, she landed at the hospital's emergency helicopter pad.

May paced between Ericka's room in the maternity ward and the waiting area across the hall. Jameson lingered near the doorway of the waiting area. She stopped and stood beside him as they focused on the TV.

"I can't believe you were able to convince that chopper pilot to take Izzy and Caledonia out to the explosion site." She looked at him. "He acted like he didn't want to get involved."

"Money speaks loudly," Jameson replied as he took her hand in his. "Especially to a sightseeing tour pilot with a family to feed. I promised him a bonus if he made sure they got back safely as well. I just wish I could've gotten a hold of my usual pilot. Guess he went off grid for the night when Charles took my helicopter."

"Thank you. I don't know what I'd do without you right now. With everything that's going on, I can't seem to think clearly."

"You don't have to, May," he assured her. "I'll take care of the crazy stuff and you make sure Ericka gets through the delivery. We're a team." He smiled. "Okay?"

"Okay," she agreed on a heavy sigh. "I just hope the girls find them."

"Me too." Jameson kissed her knuckles and she knew he did his best to soothe her rattled nerves.

The images on the television were horrendous. Several news crews were covering the explosion just this side of the Scottish border. The tag rolling across the bottom of the screen listed it as a suspicious event with uncertain ties to a possible militant or a terrorist group. She knew the truth. Leod was behind this. Fire trucks, police vehicles, ambulances and emergency crews were on site helping in the search and rescue of any survivors. To May it looked like total chaos.

It was reported that the body of an elderly gentleman had been pulled from the rubble close to where authorities believed the initial location of the blast occurred. Faces of injured people who apparently lived in this bunker society were flashed upon the screen as they were taken to safety. Desperately she searched the survivors found so far for any of the brothers, Cait or Jenny. Jenny's last text informed May she had joined in the search and rescue and would keep her abreast of the situation as much as she could.

That had been hours ago. With a heavy heart, she returned to Ericka's room. She did her best to smile but her mask was transparent and she knew it.

"Any word?" Ericka asked, then breathed as she'd been taught when a contraction hit. May took her hand. Mary acted as her birthing coach and helped her concentrate and breathe through the pain.

She and Gavin wanted so much to start the new generation of MacKinnons in the same tradition as their clan, to be born at Castle MacKinnon. Ericka had agreed with Gavin's terms as long as there was someone present with medical knowledge. She'd done her homework and found an experienced midwife who came highly recommended.

Also Gavin had to be at her side during the birth. His facial expression when Ericka mentioned this was priceless. It was a mixture of shock and apprehension that morphed into a tinge of excitement he'd tried to hide. May could still see it in her head and it made her smile. Even though he'd protested, stating *men of his time did no such thing,* he'd given in to his wife's request. As easily as he'd relented, May suspected he wouldn't have had it any other way.

May sighed, grateful the contraction passed, and Ericka released the vise-grip hold to her hand. Unfortunately part of her request didn't look as if it were going to happen. This baby wasn't going to wait to return to MacKinnon land before making its appearance. And worse, it didn't look like Gavin would be witnessing the miracle of the birth of their newest family member.

From the devastation she'd seen on the TV, she feared he wasn't going to see his child now or ever. She desperately tried to cling to a sliver of hope she was wrong, that the images flashing in her brain of the blast site were not as bad as they appeared. She struggled to remain positive for Ericka's sake. For the baby's sake.

Fate interfered. Not fate. May cringed. Brother Leod played a wicked hand and might've actually succeeded in killing the brothers where he'd failed so miserably in the past. May tried to contain the thoughts of hopelessness that all were lost. She kept a brave face for Ericka and gave her as good a smile as she could muster.

"There's been no new word as yet."

Mary looked up from under the sheet between Ericka's bended knees. "The babe's in perfect position. I know you've been holding back, resisting the urge to push, but it's time. This babe's ready."

"I don't want to push," Ericka cried. "Not without Gavin."

"If'n it be time to push, then ye push. Ye can't be keeping my wee one to yourself and not share," a male voice announced happily from the doorway. Three heads simultaneously turned in its direction. Ericka squealed in delight as a dirt-covered Gavin hurried to her bedside. "No let it be said this MacKinnon let ye down."

"Nay," Ericka mimicked his brogue, "never."

Their lips locked in a kiss as tears streamed down May's cheeks. She hated to interrupt but she desperately needed to know. She touched his shoulder. Gavin lifted from the kiss but didn't release the hug he had around his wife and met May's gaze.

"The others?"

"Are safe," Gavin informed her. "Jameson left with the twins. The sun be on the horizon. He be taking them and the young ladies to the hotel. The oth—" His sentence was stopped short when his wife dug her nails into his upper arms and groaned as a contraction hit. Immediately his attention fell to her. "Breathe, *m'gaol*—my love. Breathe." He kissed her brow and held her until the pain subsided.

"I hate to break this up but you are a dirty mess, Mr. MacKinnon," Mary stated with a shake of her head. Her thick Scottish brogue was undeniable. "This is supposed to be a clean environment for the baby's sake."

"Aye." He nodded, pulling himself away from Ericka. May pointed him to the private bathroom. He stared straight at Ericka as he spoke. "I shall only be a moment, *m'gaol*." Then he disappeared to the sound of running water from the sink.

Reassured Ericka was okay, May took a moment and went into the hall. She walked to the far end and stood near the window, looking out into the early-morning sky. Gavin's appearance was a miracle. His timing couldn't have been any better. Smiling, she pulled her cell phone from her pocket and dialed Jameson. He answered on the first ring.

"I've been expecting your call," he stated. His tone was filled with happiness. "Your present is almost safe and sound at the hotel. We'll be there within a few minutes. They should be inside before the sun rises."

"Thank you, Jameson." May smiled into the phone, even though she knew he couldn't see it. "How are the young ladies?"

"Jenny and Cait are both fine. Cait's a bit worse for wear, covered in dirt, but alive. I think after a hot bath, a good meal and a decent sleep both shall be feeling better and more able to relate what happened in greater detail. They're exhausted."

"I bet they are. Please let them know how grateful we are for their help."

"Already have," Jameson replied. "Several times."

"How are the others?" She heard him take a hesitant breath and her stomach dropped. Something was wrong.

"Padon has a few minor injuries, bumps, cuts and bruises. Struan has a possible dislocated shoulder. Izzy thinks Ian has a broken arm and ankle from their initial assessments. Apparently if it weren't for Donnell's quick thinking, they'd all be dead. But I don't have the full story as yet."

She released the breath she'd been holding, expecting far worse news. "Are they receiving medical attention in the emergency room?"

"Not at the moment." He hesitated and May immediately thought the worst. "The scenic pilot dropped the girls and took off. It was too much for him to handle. Izzy said he freaked when he saw the devastation and wanted no part of it. Charles is en route back to the site to retrieve the others. As soon as Gavin was informed Ericka was in labor, the brothers united against him and made him be on the first trip. Due to time constraints, the twins had no choice but to be on board as well. The sun plays against them right now. Ian and Struan refused medical attention at the site. Ian suggested they stay hidden until the helicopter returns. It would be too much to have to explain why they were there in the first place."

"How's the helicopter not being noticed?" She couldn't imagine it would land and take off without someone seeing it.

"May, there's so much going on there right now. Besides, there are several medevac helicopters coming and going it's probably assumed to be one of those."

From what she'd seen on the news, that was definitely a possibility. "How'd they get out?"

"Through a tunnel connecting the bunker to another bunker. Seems our infamous Brother Leod didn't make many fans with the community members when he and his band of misfits overtook their home. The community never shared all the details of the compound with them.

"We're at the hotel. I'm going to get everyone settled and fed, then I'll return to the hospital as soon as possible."

"Okay. Jameson," May said on a tired whisper, "I love you."

"I love you too, May."

Chapter Fourteen

Showered and well fed, Jenny and Cait sat on their beds dressed in new pajamas from the hotel gift shop. They had been given the room with two double beds connected to May's suite. The twins were in statue form in the sitting room and its doorway was in direct eyesight of Jenny and Cait's room. If anyone tried to enter it, they'd know, especially since Belvedere had taken to guarding that door. His bark would surely wake them. They doubted anyone would enter the suite today, since Jameson had requested total privacy from the hotel management before he left for the hospital.

"I'm so glad you're safe," Jenny said. "It had to be scary down there when it collapsed."

Cait shrugged. "I won't lie. I was scared, but the brothers gave me no chance to think about it."

"How'd they find the escape tunnel so fast?" Jenny snuggled deeper into the covers as she lay on her side facing Cait.

"We had help. One of the three men guarding us was just a kid, a teenager. Donnell knocked his uncle out when we tricked them into opening the cell door they had us captive in. I tackled the kid but the third guy disappeared. We knew he didn't go out the door we came in, so when you let Gavin know about the possibility they were lining the exit with explosives, it didn't take much to convince the kid to tell us." She grinned as if something she thought of tickled her.

"What?" Jenny questioned, rising onto her elbow.

She shook her head as she replied, "I have to admit that kid's got a lot of moxie. He stood his ground, stared Donnell right in the eye and made one demand in exchange for the exit's location."

"What was that?"

"We had to take him and his uncle with us."

"That's only fair," Jenny stated, a little taken aback they would've left the pair to be buried alive.

"Oh, we had no intention of leaving them. But someone had to carry his uncle since he wasn't exactly coherent enough to walk straight. Seems Donnell flattened him pretty hard."

"Is that how Ian got hurt? Carrying the guy?" Concern filled Jenny's tone. She'd hated leaving the injured men behind but the brothers were insistent they go on the helicopter with the twins and Gavin.

"Noooo." Cait drew the word out, then continued, "Padon carried the uncle. The kid led the way into the escape tunnel, followed by Gavin and the rest of us. Ian brought up the rear. He shut the door behind us at the same time the explosion occurred. The force pushed the door back in on him, sending him flying into Struan, who actually broke his fall. The way Ian landed on him caused Struan's shoulder dislocation. But neither of them hesitated. They immediately sprang upright and helped each other get the hell out of there."

"Ohmygod." Jenny's eyes widened.

"Those men have the biggest, baddest sets of balls I've ever known. None of the MacKinnons let the dust clear before they forced everyone to shake the dirt off and move. No one knew how badly Ian and Struan were hurt until we reached the connecting bunker on the opposite side of the compound. That's when Gavin was able to reconnect with Charles, let him know our location."

"Then Gavin contacted me," Jenny said. "I was never so glad to hear from someone before in my life. I'd made my way to the compound and with the confusion, no one noticed me. I was searching for Dour and you." She sat up, swung her legs off the bed, stood and pounced on Cait's bed. Cait sat up just in time to be hugged. "I thought I'd lost my best friend."

"You can't get rid of me that easily," Cait teased.

"I don't want to get rid of you," Jenny protested. "Who else would I have to go with on these crazy adventures?"

"Crazy adventures, huh," she replied, lifting her eyes toward the sitting room door.

Jenny followed her stare. "In that room is someone awesome," she whispered.

"A pair of awesome someones," Cait corrected as she agreed.

"Cait," Jenny said, turning her gaze back to her best friend, "I think I've fallen in love with a man who has a major issue with the sun."

She burst out laughing, causing Jenny to laugh right along with her. "I think it's more than an issue," she replied in between gasps of air, calming her laughter. "It's called a curse." She cleared her throat and held Jenny's hand. "Go figure. You and I finally find us a pair of lovable men and they turn out to be gargoyles."

They burst into laughter again. Cait slid over and Jenny lay beside her. They laughed themselves into total exhaustion amid a flood of hysterical tears.

"So what do we do about it?" Jenny questioned once she could speak.

"We use every resource we have available and find the cure to the curse."

* * * * *

"Do you think we should tell them?" Ericka asked, looking into the garden from her and Gavin's bedroom window. He moved to stand beside her.

Dour and Donnell were in statue form exactly where they'd shifted earlier that morning. Cait and Jenny sat on a blanket in between the frozen pair, sharing a picnic lunch. Jenny tapped on a laptop. Cait thumbed through a stack of books about curses she'd borrowed from Castle MacKinnon's library.

"Nay," he replied. "Ye know the rules. From the looks of what we've seen the past few nights, it won't be long before my youngest *brathairs* admit the truth of their hearts to that fine pair of lassies." He held his six-week-old son in his arms.

Ericka crossed her arms and turned to face him. Her eyebrow arched as he met her gaze.

"You know you don't have to pick him up every time he cries. You're spoiling him."

"I no be spoiling young Brady. I be protecting him from having nightmares as he sleeps." Gavin puffed his chest and grinned.

Ericka shook her head and smiled back at him. "You're impossible. We need to go downstairs to help with the final details for May's wedding. And Brady needs his nap." She patted her breasts and Gavin's eyes widened with passionate heat. "Trust me, his tummy is full, so that should give us a few good hours to accomplish something."

Gently he tucked Brady in his crib then gathered Ericka into a hug. "Do we have time to make another?" He wagged his eyebrows and Ericka giggled.

"We always have time for that."

Gavin lifted her and headed straight for the bed. "May will have to wait a wee bit more."

"Only a wee bit?" Ericka teased.

"Have I ever failed to please ye?" His voice deepened.

"Nay, *m'gaol*, never."

* * * * *

Cait and Jenny sat in the second row from the front beside Donnell and Dour. The garden was well lit with strings of bright lights everywhere and candles all around the altar. Charles acted as Jameson's best man. May's niece, Ericka, stood as matron of honor. Gavin sat in the front row holding Brady, who was dressed in a miniature kilt that matched his father's and a cute little white dress shirt.

Izzy's father, Angus MacDonell, acted as officiate for the wedding ceremony. He not only owned the local pub, Grant's Tavern, he was recently elected town mayor, which gave him the legal right to perform civil services. He stood under the arch of wildflowers and lavender with the groom, who looked tremendously happy to be waiting on his forthcoming bride. Cait couldn't help but smile at the beautiful look of anticipation on his face. She cut a sideways glance at Donnell and sighed.

Each of the MacKinnon brothers looked dapper in the family's traditional kilts. As far as she was concerned, Donnell was the handsomest. She kept catching herself staring at him dressed in full ancient regalia right down to the leather boots on his feet. His bright-red hair was pulled back in a tie at his nape. Every time he looked at her with those drop-dead-sexy green eyes, she wanted to jump his bones and kiss each and every freckle on his body, including the ones on his cock.

God, she loved this man but for some reason hadn't told him. The words just wouldn't exit her lips. They seemed lodged in her throat. Several times she'd wanted to tell him, to hear him say it back, but stopped. What if he didn't feel the same way? Would her saying it first end their relationship? When he caught her staring, she quickly darted her eyes forward. For now, she intended to be happy with the time she shared with Donnell. There was no way she was going to let a little thing like three words ruin her chances with him.

Or end the possibility of her ever having sex with him again. With the wedding being set for exactly one hour after dusk so the twins could participate, they'd barely had time for a quickie before having to be dressed and in their seats for the ceremony. Just thinking about him taking her up against the wall in the shower had her wet, willing and ready for another go. Cait took a moment to control her lust. It wasn't easy with the object of her desire sitting so close to her their thighs touched, and each time he moved he seemed to brush some part of her. Intentional or not, it was killing her.

In an attempt to think of something other than sex, she turned her focus to the people gathered for the wedding. Izzy and Ian sat in front of them. Ian had a cast on his forearm and wore a walking brace on his leg, which hadn't been broken but had a severely strained Achilles tendon and suffered bone bruising. She'd seen a picture of Izzy with short, spiked white hair but liked her current look better. Her hair was shoulder-length and its natural deep-auburn tone made her green eyes stand out. Ian had his dark hair pulled back and tied with a leather strap. Apparently he liked Izzy's longer length as well, because he kept his arm relaxed on her chair back and his fingers toyed with her hair since they'd taken their seats. Cait smiled at the affectionate touch.

In a row to the right of the center aisle sat Struan and Caledonia. This woman had the strangest color blue eyes she'd ever seen and her jet-black hair was kept in a braid that landed below her waist. Struan sat close to her. His hair was also tied back in a ponytail but this was the first time Cait noticed the streaks of red highlights in his otherwise dark hair. Behind them sat Padon and Lynn. Now, they were an adorable pair as far as she was concerned. He was tall and large with dark-auburn hair and she was short and robust in stature with a smile that never faded. Her bright-blue eyes seemed to twinkle when she looked at Padon.

The brothers were close-knit but for some reason refused to share the secret to ending the curse. Four of them were free and lived a normal life, or as normal as possible for men born hundreds of years ago, cursed and awakened to live in a totally different world. For the past six weeks, she and Jenny had done everything possible to coax the answer from any of them without success. Akira's words of advice on the matter taunted her thoughts daily. *The answer ye seek lies within one's heart.*

What the hell did that mean? She tried not to linger on it as she smiled from one person to the other as she scanned the intimate gathering.

There were only a few others in attendance. Margaret and Ned, the married couple who worked as the housekeeper and the handyman/groundskeeper. Margaret wanted to make all the food for the reception, but May insisted she relax and enjoy the wedding and had everything catered. That had been an interesting conversation to overhear, but May won in the end. Cait smiled remembering the gentle way May convinced the older woman she wanted her included in the festivities as her friend.

Izzy's best friends, Nessia MacKay and Colin Campbell, sat side by side and were an obvious couple, though they pretended not to be. Cait shook her head at that one. Caledonia's parents, Mr. and Mrs. Kavanaugh, and her two closest friends, the O'Reilly brothers, Abel and Percy, sat together. Friends of Lynn and Padon, Travis Shain and Fin MacIntyre, along with Fin's grandfather, Thicket MacIntyre, sat in the last row of chairs.

Now that Thicket MacIntyre might be a good match for her Gran. Cait shook her head. Matchmaking. What the hell was she thinking? It had to be the wedding scene that had her mind working that way. Her Gran had loved meeting everyone when she visited the week before and it didn't surprise Cait she understood the curse thing and the clan. Gran was special that way. It disappointed Cait that Gran couldn't make it to the wedding. She had prior plans.

When the music started and May stepped into sight at the far end of the center aisle. Akira floated at her side. Being the only MacKinnon sister, she was spared the curse. If it weren't for her efforts, Hume MacGillivray would've destroyed the MacKinnon brothers as they slept in statue form. For a split second, Cait truly hated MacGillivray for what he'd done but if he hadn't, she wouldn't have Donnell.

She slid her hand into his as they stood. He smiled at her, and her insides heated. Damn. She liked when he looked at her like that, as if he wanted to kiss her. Cait broke eye contact with him and lifted her gaze to the bride. Belvedere led the way wearing a bright-green bowtie and a matching top hat. When they reached the altar, Akira gave her away, then floated to hover beside Ericka. Belvedere sat at Angus MacDonnell's side, facing the audience as if it were his job to oversee everything and make sure it went right.

The ceremony was short and beautiful. The vows they'd written left not a dry eye among the women. May and Jameson were the perfect couple. Smiles were permanently glued to their faces at the reception, which was held in the huge common room of Castle MacKinnon. A buffet table of food lined one side of the room. A local band was in the back corner and played traditional wedding music. A dance floor had been placed beside the band. May and Jameson had the tables arranged in a circle at one end of the room with their table in the middle. They wanted to be able to share every joyous moment with everyone.

Donnell took her hand and led her to the dance floor. He whispered, "I am not much of a dancer but with a lady as beautiful as ye upon my arm, I refuse not to at least try."

Cait smiled at him. After a few minutes, she realized he wasn't lying, so before it cost her some toes, she nodded toward the door leading to the garden. "I could use some air."

They crossed the hall and out through the double glass doors leading into the rear garden. A full moon gave tremendous light, showing the pathways with ease. The side garden was where the ceremony had been held. This garden was Cait's favorite. She and Jenny spent many hours researching the curse with no luck of finding a cure, while tucked away on a lawn hidden within this maze of shrubs, flowers and trees. In the center was a water fountain with benches nestled in alcoves of shrubbery around it. Out the rear gate led into a field of wildflowers and lavender, something she wished she could share with Donnell since it was her favorite spot she'd found so far on MacKinnon land.

A movement caught her eye and she turned just in the nick of time to see Dour and Jenny kissing as he walked her backward into the trees and out of sight. She smiled, knowing Jenny was in love and from the look on Dour's face recently, she didn't doubt he felt the same about her. Lucky girl. She didn't get the chance to think on it before Donnell clasped her elbow and spun her into his arms.

His lips met hers and all thought of what anyone else was doing dissipated instantly. The heat of his hands skimming along her arms gave her chills. When he cupped her arse and tugged her close, the hardness beneath his kilt couldn't be missed. His warm breath tickled her ear as he whispered, "*Mi brèagha neamhnaid*, I have been in need of ye in my arms. The shower only whetted my appetite for ye."

It was wonderfully arousing to know he wanted her as much as she wanted him. And every time he called her his pretty pearl it made her heart swell. Never had anyone given her a pet name. In any other situation, she probably wouldn't have liked it, but with Donnell it seemed natural, and the way he spoke it gave her chills and made her hot at the same time.

She stretched upward for another kiss but froze at the sound of a woman's scream. Donnell spun around, as did she, trying to determine the direction from which it came. In a flash, he removed the *sgian dubh* — dagger — from its sheath hidden inside his boot. With her hand in his, they followed the sound of voices arguing on the other side of the hedge. At the opening into that pathway, they met Dour and Jenny doing the same thing, tracking the sound of the voices. Dour held a dagger similar to the one Donnell carried. The brothers nodded to one another.

"Stay here," Dour whispered to the women.

As soon as they stepped a few feet away, Cait turned to Jenny and nodded in their direction. The pair silently followed the men. The voices grew louder. Cait recognized Struan's deep timbre. He sounded calm yet intimidating, warning someone not to harm his woman. Someone threatened Caledonia? Who? Why?

Where the path opened into another hidden alcove containing a small fishpond with a bench beside it, she noted Dour and Donnell split up. Each slid into the shadows of the trees surrounding the area and she guessed they were angling for better positions to help.

Slowly she and Jenny stepped closer, making sure not to be seen. She kept Jenny behind her as they eased to one side of the path and lingered in the darkness provided by the shrubs and trees. Carefully Cait peeked through the branches. She'd be damned. That rat from the warehouse stood holding a knife to Caledonia's neck. The last she'd heard of him, he'd still been in the hospital awaiting release to jail, but that was weeks ago. How the hell had he managed to escape?

"Kip, why are you doing this?" Cait heard the desperation in Caledonia's voice. Moonlight glinted off the steel at her neck.

"You belong to me," he growled loudly. His voice cracked and his hand shook dangerously closer to Caledonia's skin. "Not to statue boy there."

Struan took a step but froze when Kip dug the tip into her flesh to make a point. "Not a step closer, asshole," Kip yelled. His hand fisted Caledonia's braid and jerked her head backward, tightening the skin of her neck, making it the perfect cutting board.

"Caledonia does not belong to ye, Crosby," Struan spat angrily at the dirty, smaller man. Cait saw his one fist ball and unball at his side. His other arm remained in a sling, keeping his shoulder intact. She doubted that would stop him from using it in a fight. She could tell he was calculating his next move carefully so as not to spill Caledonia's blood. "She be no man's possession. She be a woman with a mind of her own and she chose me over ye."

"She is mine. Together we'll rise to the top of the treasure-hunting world. And you," he gasped, "you'll be a forgotten memory once Brother Leod has his way with you and your whole clan."

Kip tugged Caledonia by the braid, making her walk as he walked, moving toward the pathway. Struan moved in sync, never taking his eyes off the intruder. Realizing he was headed her way, Cait took the opportunity being handed to her. The MacKinnon men needed a distraction and she had just the thing. As subtly as possible, she slid the emergency kit out of her bra, because in the dress she wore there was nowhere else to keep it and she never went anywhere unprepared.

A smile split her lips as she lit the firecracker's fuse, waited a second for him to take one more step closer, then threw it to land directly behind him at his feet. Never had she seen anyone jump so high or heard a man scream in such a high-pitched tone to the point you would've thought she'd shot him. He dropped the knife from Caledonia's throat and it was all Struan needed to take him down. He wasn't alone in his efforts. Caledonia elbowed Kip in the ribs and jerked free of his weakened grip just as Struan made contact with a solid blow to his jaw. Kip's head twisted to the side. The knife went flying into the trees. Dour and Donnell lunged from their positions, *sgian dubhs* poised at the ready.

Kip slowly folded to his knees. His head wobbled on his shoulders like a bobble-head doll. Dour looked at Donnell, then gave a shove to Kip's back with a swift kick of his booted foot. The man fell face forward into the grass.

"So he was stupid enough to come here after all," May exclaimed as almost everyone from the wedding rushed onto the scene.

"You knew he escaped?" Cait asked.

She nodded. "We were informed by the authorities Kip Crosby managed to get away. From what they've determined, a thug named Roy Finnegan dressed as a male nurse got into Crosby's room, apparently with the intent to kill him. There was a scuffle between them, which alerted the guards outside the room. During the chaos of them trying to apprehend this Roy guy, Crosby exited the room and the hospital."

"Why did he come here?" Jenny asked, stepping out of the shadows to stand beside Dour. "Why did he want to hurt Caledonia?"

"He's my ex-husband," Caledonia explained. "He used to be such a wonderful person until greed took over his soul. He blames me for his being arrested. You see, when I brought Struan up from the bottom of the loch, he stole Struan in statue form, thinking he'd make a lot of money selling him on the black market. Trouble was, I had no plans of losing Struan. We followed him and took Struan back." She shook her head. "Even though we knew Kip escaped, I'd hoped he wouldn't try anything. I was wrong."

Struan wrapped his good arm around her, hugging her tight. "*Mi fiadh-cat* — wildcat — it be over. He won't get away this time."

Ian hobbled onto the scene along with Izzy. "*Och.* I missed the fun," he grumbled. "Damn boot. It be slowing me down."

"Good thing," Izzy teased. "You might've gotten in the way. Looks like your brothers handled it just fine."

"Ye be right," he admitted as he leaned closer to Izzy. "I can think of other ways to be having a bit of fun." Izzy just grinned at him.

As he reached the group, Charles said, "When I saw you gentlemen had it under control, I called the authorities. They're on the way." He tossed a roll of thick gray tape to Donnell. "I grabbed this from the kitchen drawer. Bind his ankles and wrists together with it. It'll hold him until they arrive to take him away."

From the bunched-brow look on his face, Cait knew he didn't understand the substance he held in his hands. She took it from him and pulled a long piece free from the roll. "It's called tape. It's sticky and has a world of wonderful uses."

She straddled the facedown man, bent over, grabbed his ankles and wound the strip around them tightly. When she turned to obtain more, she wasn't surprised to see Donnell doing the same to his wrists. She shot him a wink and teased, "I knew you were a fast learner."

He grinned, leaning close to her as he whispered, "I could think of a few good uses for this later." Then he wagged his eyebrows and she knew she blushed from the heat seeping up her neck to fill her cheeks. His grin broadened as he helped her step over Kip.

The O'Reillys offered to move him to the front and watch over him until the authorities arrived. They dragged him a few feet, letting his head bounce until Caledonia stepped in.

"As much as I know he doesn't deserve any kindness, please don't break his neck or bash his skull by moving him like that."

"Aww, Cali," Percy O'Reilly groaned in a teasing manner, "we never get to have any fun."

Abel nudged his brother, leaned in and whispered loudly, "We just have to carry him until she can't see us anymore, then we can let him taste the dirt of the motherland again."

Caledonia crossed her arms over her chest and gave them a raised-eyebrow look. "I heard that. Don't make me follow you all the way around the castle to the driveway."

Cait snickered at the bickering threesome. Those two might not be her blood brothers but they sure acted like true siblings in her book. Struan stepped forward, reached down with his good arm and grabbed a handful of Crosby's hair.

"Come on, lads," he announced with a mischievous grin. "I'll be glad to help carry him."

Jameson stated loudly, "Show's over. Let's get this party started again."

"I agree." May kissed his cheek and held his hand as he led them back inside.

Chapter Fifteen

"It's never a dull moment with this clan," Jenny claimed as Dour led her to the dance floor.

One arm wrapped around her waist while his other hand held hers snugly against his chest in between them. "Would ye prefer dull?" His brows bunched as he met her gaze.

She liked the teasing look he gave her. His eyes darkened and his lips twisted into a sensual smile. Damn. He melted her insides when he looked at her like that, as if he wanted to ravish her at any moment. Jenny stretched upward until her lips hovered close to his.

"You couldn't be dull even if you tried." She sealed her words with a kiss.

Dour parted their lips, holding his forehead to hers, he gave her an invitation she couldn't resist. "What say ye to us slipping upstairs and me showing ye how non-dull I can be?"

Jenny grinned. "I'd like that." She looked around. "You think anyone would notice us being gone?"

"Nay," he replied, slowly dancing her toward the main hallway. "We be the least of their concerns."

He twirled her out the door and without a second thought they scurried upstairs to Dour's chambers. Jenny liked the fact each of the brothers had their own section within the castle. It gave them privacy when they wanted. The center tower belonged to Gavin and Ericka. From Jenny's understanding, its renovations had been stalled by Akira as she protected Gavin. They had only recently moved into it upon completion of its updates.

Every time the castle changed hands, Akira kept them from making any changes to that tower. She haunted it, caused accidents to workers and scared everyone to the point one set of owners closed off the center tower and renovated around it. Since moving into the castle and becoming friends with Akira, Jenny understood Akira's fiercely protective nature. She could see her doing whatever it took to prevent Gavin's tower from being transformed and his statue being discovered by the wrong person. It wasn't until May bought the castle that Akira allowed Gavin to be found by Ericka. Jenny couldn't help but smile, thinking of the happy couple and their baby boy.

She ticked off the locations of each family member in her head. Ian and Izzy had the east corner tower. Struan and Caledonia lived in the south corner tower. Padon and Lynn moved into the west corner tower. The north corner tower belonged to the missing brother, Aiden, and remained unoccupied. That was temporary as far as they all were concerned. Donnell and Dour had substantial chambers within different wings of the castle.

The closeness of this family reminded her of her own brothers, which made her smile widen. It had been one interesting phone call she'd made home, explaining she and Cait had made some new friends. She'd left out the parts about the abduction and the explosion and most of the entire curse thing. She doubted they'd understand or believe the truth about the MacKinnon clan so she'd thought it best to leave it out of the conversation. She did share the job offer May presented to her and Cait.

It made her mother very happy to learn she now had a steady income working with May's company, The Center for the Restoration of Folklore and Mythology. Helping locate the last brother was the first priority at the moment. What sealed the deal as far as she and Cait were concerned, it kept them close to Dour and Donnell and even allowed them to continue their online magazine.

Living at the castle was better than the tiny flat in London. She liked that Dour's chambers faced the east. The morning sun filtered in through their bedroom window, bringing her a new hope each day she'd find the answer to the curse and free him forever. It just burned her biscuits to think the brothers knew the way to freedom and refused to share. There had to be a reason. They weren't the kind to be intentionally mean. Jenny pushed the thoughts to the back of her mind. Now wasn't the time to think on it.

She knew the truth of her heart and planned to share it with him this night. Could it have been the soul-touching vows May and Jameson shared during their wedding that had her thinking of a future with Dour? Maybe it had tipped the scales for her but she didn't care. Looking at him, she knew every second spent with Dour was phenomenal and she was determined to have as many special moments with him as humanly possible.

If she'd learned anything from her brothers, it was to go for what she wanted and worry about the consequences later. Lord knew they'd done that more times than she could count. Thinking about their escapades gave her comfort. They'd made her strong even though they'd been overprotective. One thing she did know—Dour was going to fit right in with her crew of mischief-makers. He and Donnell had proven over the past few weeks, if there was a practical joke pulled, they were behind it, especially for poor Ian. Jenny grinned at Dour. Yep. He was going to fit right in.

When they reached the chamber door, he pushed it open and stood staring in for a second and she knew he was still hesitant over the changes to the castle. It had taken Jenny hours of explaining to bring Dour up to date on some of today's conveniences. Electricity floored him. He still tended to play with the switch, flipping it up and down several times, watching in amazement as the lights went on and off. It was the bathroom he liked the most, especially the oversized tub. According to him it was perfectly built for two and they'd tested that theory on more than one occasion. She wasn't sure she'd ever want to bathe alone again.

Without warning, he scooped her into his arms and carried her through the door. He shoved it shut with the heel of his boot. Jenny couldn't help but laugh. His touch and the warmth of being near him made her happier than she ever thought possible.

"Milady, ye be beautifully clothed this evening," he stated as he marched them straight to the bed. "But it be your body I wish to see. Ye have had me wanting for a taste of ye since I woke."

Slowly she slid down the length of him, enjoying the feel of his abdominal muscles against her side. She stood between him and the bed. He looked strikingly handsome in his off-white dress shirt, kilt of the MacKinnon red-and-green plaid, and black boots. One by one, she unbuttoned his shirt, planting tender kisses to his flesh as it appeared.

"I have to say," she stated breathily as she sank to her knees, untucking his shirt as she went. "You are the most beautiful man I've ever met."

He laughed huskily. "Milady, me thinks ye have misspoken. Men be not beautiful. Not like a woman with her lovely curves, wondrous smile and eyes of the deepest green." He paused as his hands slid into her updo, working it free of its pins. "And hair as soft as the finest silk."

Jenny's insides fluttered. She loved it when he spoke poetically. No one she'd dated of this time ever said such things to her. It seemed so natural coming from his lips, not forced as if he were trying to impress her to get her into bed. His thick Scottish brogue made each word twice as sensual. They'd spent the last six weeks getting to know one another and she'd treasured every second of their precious time, every sexual escapade and adventure he'd taken her on to the point she couldn't imagine life without him. She didn't want to think of anything else but being with him, even if it meant sleeping during the day to be awake with him at night.

"No," she replied, holding his gaze. She watched it darken as she lifted his kilt. "What I spoke was truth." Doing her best to mimic his brogue, she added, "Milord, ye doth have the most beautiful cock."

Ducking under his kilt, she licked his length from tip to base and back. She held his shaft in her hand while massaging his balls with the other as her tongue lavished the slender opening of its head, tasting the salt of his pre-cum. His was a flavor she hungered to devour. Dour was her man and she intended to show him how much she loved him. Jenny sucked the head, twirling her tongue around it in a gentle tease.

His moan was muffled by the kilt, which didn't last but a few moments before it disappeared from around her. He unwrapped it from his waist and tossed it to the floor. Jenny met his heated gaze as his hands plowed into her hair.

Desperation tinged his tone. "I had to see ye as ye tasted my shaft. It be a glorious sight, your lips to my flesh. One I no wished to miss."

That was all she needed to hear to spur her on with the task of pleasuring him. His hands cradled her head, not pushing her, not forcing her to take him in farther than her mouth allowed. She liked the fact he let her set the pace. Slowly she slid him in deeper until she could take no more. Over and over she pumped as he massaged her scalp. His breathing increased and his balls tightened and she knew he was close. Suddenly he pulled her from him and dragged her to her feet. His mouth found hers in a passionate kiss.

He grappled with her dress as they fell upon the bed, tangled together. "I need to be inside ye, Jenny."

Her dress bunched around her waist. She arched, lifting her hips, giving him room to tug the sexy panties down. In his rush, Dour ripped them off her seconds before he entered her. "Dour," she gasped as she wrapped her legs around his waist and twisted her fingers into the long strands of his red hair.

Setting a sensually slow rhythm, he stroked her. He held his weight on his forearms, his hands on either side of her face. "Now this be heaven," he whispered as he captured her mouth.

He wanted nothing more than to stay in this position forever. Jenny's legs hugged him tight, keeping him snugly encased in her sheath. Her mouth fit his perfectly for kissing. He liked the way her tongue toyed with his. The way she'd pleasured his shaft had him on edge to the point he had to be inside her or be spent in her mouth. Though it was a wonderful way to reach his release, he would much rather share the sensation with his woman.

The thought hit him mid-stroke and he stalled for a second before she dug her heels into his backside, urging him to keep the rhythm. Dour broke from the kiss. He locked his gaze on hers. Heavy lids held at half-mast nearly hid those sexy greens from view. Her sighs were the only music he longed to hear. It made him increase his speed, pumping into her a notch faster. It was all he could do not to increase too hard and fast. He wanted it to last, to draw out this moment.

Jenny was his woman. He liked the sound of that as it rolled through his brain. She was his and he intended to show her how much he desired her, wanted her in his bed now and forever. Forever. How could he ask a woman to be with him when it meant living a half-life? Man by night and stone by day.

Her nails dragged down his spine underneath his shirt. The spark of pain added to his pleasure, causing him to spike into her.

"Yes," she gasped. "Harder, Dour. Harder, baby."

The feel of her sheath contracting around him nearly undid him but he refused to reach his release. Not until Jenny reached the same point in their combined pleasure. Never before had he been so concerned over the woman reaching release along with him. Every time he and Jenny coupled, it mattered. It wasn't about him and his bawls being drained. It was about her. He wanted her to be satisfied.

Dour's heart thumped ready to burst with the love he finally admitted he felt for the vixen beneath him. He slowed the action and her eyes opened wide, letting him know he had her full attention. Cupping her face in his hands, he stared directly into her gaze. He didn't want her to miss one word he had to say.

"Jenny, *mi milis subh-làir* — sweet strawberry, I should nay be saying this with naught more to offer ye than my presence in your life at night." He gathered his courage, then continued before he thought better of it. "I love ye."

Her eyes widened and she stilled beneath him. For a split second he wished he hadn't said it because it didn't seem to bode well with her. Instantly her face changed. The biggest smile he'd ever seen lifted her lips as her arms snaked around his neck.

"I love you too, Dour." Jenny kissed him. Her legs slid from around his waist and hovered bent at his sides. He felt her feet plant into the bed as she did a slow rock along him. Her hand fisted his hair and a devilish gleam filled her eyes. "I do believe I told you I wanted it harder."

He grinned, knowing he'd made no mistake in speaking the truth of his heart to this one. She was meant to be his and he hers. "As ye wish, *mi milis subh-làir*."

Dour drove into her, relishing the grasp of her sheath to his shaft. Slick heat coated his flesh, coaxing him to increase his pace. Her moans lifted to his ears, letting him know she enjoyed this as much as he. When he nuzzled her breasts, it impressed him how quickly she undid the clasp of her halter-style dress, loosening the material for him without skipping a beat in their rhythm. Using his teeth he uncovered a nipple ripe for him to suck.

He nibbled the taut bud and she squealed in delight. Her hands held his head in place, urging him to continue. He sucked and nipped the tender flesh of her breast as he increased the pace. She met him pump for pump. He loved her reaction each time he captured her nipple between his teeth and tugged. Moisture coated him and she practically growled. Her fingers twisted tighter in his hair.

She had him teetering on the edge and he was ready to take the free fall into pure pleasure with his woman. Dour broke from the grip she had in his hair to take command of her lips. He speared into her hard and fast. He left her lips and sucked her neck, leaving hot kisses all over her flesh. Gasping for air, he met her gaze.

"Come with me, *m'gaol*—my love. Make me whole."

Once again her legs wrapped tightly around his waist, causing him to sink even deeper into her. The tightening of her sheath grasping him was his undoing. Liquid heat spurted from him, mixing with her essence as their pleasure overtook them. After several long moments lying entangled, he opened his eyes and looked into hers.

"Aye, this surely be heaven."

He kissed her as they snuggled on top of the covers, lingering in the warmth of the afterglow. This was his woman. She'd accepted him as he was—cursed. They lay for hours kissing and making love, knowing the sun would soon separate them.

Dour stood and held his hand to her. "Come, Jenny. Let me turn down the covers and make you comfortable before the curse takes me."

She did as he requested. Their clothes were long forgotten in a pile on the floor. She was beautifully naked before him. Dour hugged her close, then turned and straightened the unkempt bed. Hours of making love upon it had made it slightly disheveled. He guided her under the covers. With the suns ominous rays threatening to peek into their room, he started to move, distancing himself from her.

She refused to let him. Jenny clasped on to his arm. Her sleepy-eyed request broke his heart. "Don't go. Stay here with me."

"Ye know I cannot," he replied sadly.

She lifted onto her knees facing him as he stood beside the bed. Her arms wrapped around his waist, she held him tightly to her. "Then kiss me like you'll miss me."

Dour plowed his hand into her hair, cupped the back of her head and planted a kiss neither of them would soon forget. Her arms locked around him. He knew he should separate, not take a chance she'd turn to stone with him should they be touching when the curse took him. He pulled from her lips mere seconds before the sun glistened through the curtains. It danced across his skin as he tried to pry her hands from him, panicking she'd be cursed as well.

Fire brewed within his chest. His heart felt as if it were caught in a deadly grip. Pain ripped through him as he stumbled out of Jenny's reach. He couldn't breathe. Sweat rolled off him. Dour fell to his knees, clutching his chest and fighting for air. The second her arms were around him, he screamed and tried to push her away.

"No. No. Jenny. The curse."

She fought his efforts. Her words touched his ears and warmed his soul.

"It appears as if the curse is broken. Open your eyes, Dour. Look at me." He did as she asked. The most wonderful sight sat on her knees before him.

Jenny naked in the morning light.

Chapter Sixteen

Cait woke the next morning, stretched and rolled over to stare at the empty spot in the bed beside her. She sighed disappointedly. Every time she fell asleep in Donnell's arms, he made sure to slip out of bed before the curse took him. Neither of them knew if him touching her when it happened would cause her to turn to stone for the day as well. Donnell took every precaution to not test the theory.

In his words, it would torment his soul to know his touch brought her agony in the form of suffering the curse along with him.

Looking at him standing beside the bed hurt her heart. She got out of bed and stood naked in front of him. Gently she stroked his cheek, hoping he somehow knew she was there.

"Donnell, what are we going to do about this damn curse?" Shaking her head, she leaned against him, hugging him, desperately wanting to feel his arms wrapped around her.

On tiptoe, she kissed his lips, then halfheartedly walked to the bathroom to shower and dress. When she arrived at the door from the kitchen to the veranda, she froze. Her jaw dropped and her eyes widened.

Dour stood in the sunlight, preparing a plate of food from the sideboard. When he turned to hand it to Jenny, he leaned and gave her a kiss. Cait stumbled through the screen door.

"How?" she gasped as she rushed toward them. She touched his arm and pleaded, "How did you do this? How did you break the curse?"

"Milady Cait, I know not the answer." The smile washed from his face and his tone turned somber as his gaze lifted to the doorway. "I see ye but no Donnell. I thought surely since I be free he would be as well."

"He's still a gargoyle," she snapped angrily. She spun and grabbed Jenny by both arms, causing her to drop the plate. It shattered, sending food all over the ground. "How did you free him? What do I have to do to save Donnell?"

Jenny's eyes filled with tears as she replied, "I'm not sure. I have no clue how to set Dour free. It just happened."

She tightened her grip on Jenny's arms and shook her. "You're lying. It's not fair. Tell me what you did."

Dour grabbed Cait, jerking her away from Jenny. "Ye are out of line, Cait. Ye need to calm yourself. Ye will not be hurting Jenny because of this. If ye need to hit someone then ye can hit me."

The second he let go of her arms Cait slapped him with every ounce of anger she could muster. Tears flowed as she exited the gate and ran across the field. Frustration drove her up the high hill. She didn't care how far she went or where this path led. She just wanted to be as far away from Jenny as possible right now.

When she couldn't catch her breath, she sank to the ground, rolled onto her side and cried. Deep, soul-wrenching sobs poured freely from her. This wasn't right. This wasn't fair. Why Dour and not Donnell? And what made it worse, Jenny wouldn't share the secret of freeing the man she loved.

She didn't know how long she cried. When the tears finally subsided, she knew she wasn't alone. The sense someone watched her made her gut knot with fear. After last night's adventure with Crosby, there was no telling who might be lingering near, waiting for their chance to attack a MacKinnon or anyone in their company, and she was out of firecrackers.

"Feel no fear in my presence, Cait."

A cool sensation floated down her arm. Cait turned her head to see Akira hovered near, stroking her hand along Cait's skin. She smiled at Cait. As Cait moved into a seated position, Akira spoke.

"I come here often when I need to seek my inner peace. He was my rock, the foundation of my strength." Cait followed the spirit's hand as it guided across the huge standing headstone. Though years weathered the marble, the names and dates were still legible.

Malcolm MacDonnell

1717-1768

Akira MacDonnell

1718-1788

Cait scrambled backward. "I meant no disrespect. I didn't know this was your grave." She looked around and realized in her state of distress she'd stumbled into the MacKinnon family graveyard.

"None taken," Akira replied. She settled on the ground beside Cait. "Seems ye have had a bit of a rough start to your day."

Cait shrugged. "You could say that."

Those piercing green eyes of hers stared directly at Cait. "Jenny did not lie to ye. She truly does not understand as yet how she set Dour free."

"But you do," Cait asked. "Don't you?"

"Aye," Akira replied. "But if'n I share it with ye, it will not work. When the time be right, ye will set Donnell free. Search your heart. The answer ye seek lies within."

Before she could ask anything else, Akira disappeared. "Grr," Cait groaned in frustration as she fell back onto the grass, staring at the sky. "Why can't anybody just give a straight answer?"

She lay there thinking for several hours. Noon came and went and still she had no clear answer. The one thing she knew for sure was she needed to apologize to Jenny. It wasn't Jenny's fault she was too thickheaded to decipher the clues that had to be right in front of her face. Somehow Jenny succeeded. It was late afternoon by the time she found the courage to face her stupidity.

Her feet were heavy as lead as she took the slow walk back to the castle. She'd made a fool of herself and hurt her best friend in the process. In a few hours it would be dusk and Donnell would be awake to learn the truth of his twin's release into freedom from the curse. How would he react when he discovered she failed where Jenny succeeded for Dour?

Cait shook her head. She refused to think on that at the moment. Rescuing her friendship with Jenny was her first concern. When she reached the castle, she entered quietly through the kitchen. Margaret informed her where Jenny could be found. The family had gathered in the great room to celebrate Dour's release.

She stood in the doorway, silently watching the couples. None noticed her as she hovered, simply soaking in the view and putting two and two together. Ericka freed Gavin and now they were married and had a beautiful baby boy. Izzy freed Ian and it was obvious by the way they couldn't keep their hands off each other how they felt. Caledonia and Struan were snuggled close and he kept whispering in her ear, which made her smile, lean back and kiss him. Lynn and Padon were the quieter of the couples but there was no missing the connection between them.

May and Jameson sat smiling and happily cuddling. Being newlyweds looked good on them. They'd vowed to find the last brother before taking a honeymoon. That was the only present they wanted, to complete the MacKinnon clan.

When her gaze landed on Jenny, she looked over to the doorway as if she knew Cait stood in the shadows. Dour had his arm around her and the look on his face told Cait all she needed to know. Jenny stood and walked over to Cait.

"I'm so sorry, Jenny," Cait said, taking Jenny's hands in hers. Staring into Jenny's eyes she saw the truth and knew she was right in what she was now thinking. "Please forgive me."

"There's nothing to forgive," Jenny said. "Come join us. We're celebrating."

"I can't." Cait shook her head. "There's something I've got to do."

Jenny pulled her into a hug and whispered in her ear, "Follow your heart. The truth will set him free."

Cait stepped from the hug and smiled. "I know."

She turned on her heels and darted down the hall to the stairs. There was something she had to do and she wanted to make sure everything was perfect when she did it.

* * * * *

Dusk couldn't come fast enough. She spent the hours making everything ready for his awakening. A table loaded with a variety of food was in the sitting room of their bedchamber. The wine he liked sat opened on the nightstand beside two waiting glasses. She sat on the bed's edge, shower fresh and in a sheer, light-blue negligee that tied closed with a silk lace bow at her breasts. Foregoing the matching panties, she hoped he appreciated the easy access and peek-a-boo appeal of the lacy fringe of the negligee, which barely covered her bottom.

The second the sun disappeared, electrified static skittered across her skin. The floor vibrated and his statue cracked. He was coming free of his shell. Donnell shook the dust and pebbles from his hair and body. He looked gloriously sexy naked. Those brilliant green eyes of his darkened with lust the moment they focused on her.

Vulnerability slithered through her veins. What if she was wrong? Cait swallowed hard and steeled her resolve. She was going through with her plans and if it didn't work… Cait ignored the sudden pain in her gut. She'd deal with the outcome no matter what happened.

Donnell closed the distance, placed his palms flat on the bed on either side of her, then gently kissed her. His warm breath caressed her lips as he spoke. "Ye are a vision of pure beauty to my eyes."

Her nipples hardened and it was all she could do not to pull him down on the bed and attack him. But she had a plan and she desperately wanted to stick to it. *Woo the man* whispered through her head, *win his heart*. Her hand trembled as she placed it against the center of his chest and gave a playful push.

"You, my lover, need a bath." She stood, causing him to step back just enough for her to gain her balance. Cait gathered his hand in hers and led him toward the connecting bathroom.

He frowned. "Me being a bit dirty never bothered ye before."

She shot him a coy smile across her shoulder. "Tonight is different. I want to please you in every way I know how."

Donnell grinned. "Ye have never failed to please me ever." When he tried to tug her close, she resisted and swatted his arm for the effort.

"Behave," she commanded.

"I don't want to," he whined in a jesting manner. The distraught, boyish look upon his face made her insides melt but she forced herself to stay on course.

A dozen vanilla-scented candles lit the room. A prepared bath waited in the oversized tub. Steam rose from the water. At the tub's side, she faced him and smiled. "Your bath awaits, milord."

Cait guided him in as carefully as possible without getting wet in the process.

"Seems *mi brèagha neamhnaid* has a bit of romance in mind," Donnell stated, looking about the room as he settled in the tub. The passionate heat in his gaze nearly sizzled her soul to a crisp and made her wet, weakening her determination. "Will ye be joining me?" He held his hand to her.

She dug deep and forced her voice to work and her body to stay put. "No. I wish to please you. Now sit still and let me wash you."

His pout made her giggle and was hard to resist but she somehow managed. Cait lifted the rag and gently caressed his shoulder, then traveled across his chest, squeezing the cloth, letting the water trickle down the center between his nipples. The pert round nubs beaded into hard points. It was obvious he liked being washed. Cait filled the cloth with lavender-scented soap and followed the same path, removing dirt and grime from his flesh.

Carefully she washed his face. With his eyes closed, he couldn't see she was making sure she didn't miss cleaning every freckle. She moved to his back, making him lean forward. The broad expanse of muscles stretched and flexed, making her smile. He was doing that deliberately to turn her on and she knew it. He twitched when she washed under his arms and the bottoms of his feet. She loved the fact he was ticklish.

Donnell was nothing more than an overgrown boy with a devilishly playful streak. That was one of the features she loved about him. If she weren't careful, he'd probably pull her into the tub and ruin her plans. Cait took precautions not to let that happen. She kept his hands in sight as she continued to bathe him. She soaked his hair with several cups full of water until it was thoroughly wet. This was the task that took the longest. His hair was thick but she enjoyed washing it. Gently she massaged his scalp and he sank into a more relaxed position with his head resting in her hands. A soft moan escaped his lips and she couldn't help but grin.

Once she was certain she'd removed every ounce of dirt and debris, she whispered in his ear, "Dunk under the water and rinse the soap from your hair, please."

He slowly sank as she commanded. Suds floated in the water, haloing his head. Long strands of red hair tangled in her fingers as she helped remove the soap. The sight of his shaft standing erect in the water dried her mouth. Damn, she hadn't washed that yet.

She worked her fingers free of his hair and soaped the cloth as he surfaced. Before he had a chance to catch a full breath she was washing his erection and balls. Donnell gulped loudly and she laughed. She literally had him in the palm of her hand where she wanted him. He leaned back, lifting his hips, giving her better access.

"Ye keep that up and my pleasure will be in your hands without a doubt, milady," he said in a raspy, strained tone. She knew he was on the verge of coming.

Cait shifted into a better position on her knees, leaned over the tub and pulled the plug, letting the water drain. Holding him in her hands she shot him a sideways sexy look as she said, "Today is all about pleasure. Starting right now."

The moment the water was low enough, she took the plump head in her mouth and heard his audible hiss of enjoyment. She knew he liked it when she sucked him. At this angle it was difficult to take him in too deeply but she did her best—licking and sucking, sliding up and down, teasing the rim of the head with the tip of her tongue. Knowing what did him in, she grasped his balls in one hand while gripping the base in the other. She flicked the slit with her tongue while tenderly scratching the sensitive skin underneath his sac.

The groan rumbled up his throat and growled across lips as he lost control. His cock shivered and his balls tightened. Cait sucked the head into her mouth as warm liquid coated her tongue. Mmm. She loved his salty flavor. She drank from him until he had no more to offer. Cait wiped her mouth with the cloth and laid it neatly on the side of the tub.

She stood, retrieved the extra-large bath towel and held it wide as she smiled at him. "Milord, your evening has only begun. Please stand so I may dry you."

Donnell stood. His legs were weak but his spirit was set on high. Waking to find Cait dressed for sex gave him an immediate hard-on. Smiling at her while she gently caressed his flesh with the towel, he didn't know what game she played but he had no complaints. His fingers itched to twist in the tie at her breasts and unleash the pair of her attributes he loved to fondle. The sight of her nipples brushing the see-through material heated his blood and kept his need for her at the forefront of his mind.

Though his shaft was temporarily at rest, he knew a few moments in her talented hands and he'd be ready to slide between her thighs and pleasure her all night if she so wished. When she cupped his balls with the towel, he plowed his hand in her hair and leaned in for a kiss, not giving her a chance to pull away. He took a quick taste of her lips.

"I hunger to be sheathed within your haven, *mi brèagha neamhnaid.* Visions of ye naked kept me sane whilst the curse bound me." He hovered close to her face, holding her gaze with his. "Care to bind me to the bed with your voluptuous body and let me pleasure ye 'til ye scream my name?"

Her eyes shone with desire and he thought he'd convinced her to take him to bed. Then she added a twist to the erotic game she'd set in motion with the bath and her skilled mouth.

"The binding, as you put it, shall come later." She dropped the towel, spun on her heels and marched toward the exit. In the doorway, she shot him a look that stirred his loins as she spoke in a husky tone while wiggling her finger, motioning for him to follow. "I've got plans for you, big boy." Then she disappeared out the door.

Donnell hurried after her. He held his hands palm open, trying to feel her luscious bare bottom as he closed the distance but she managed to stay one step out of reach. She led him through the bedroom into the sitting room.

Each of the brothers had his own bedchamber, but the night they were cursed, he and Dour had lain down drunk on mats in a room on the first floor, unable to make it upstairs. The thought hit his brain for an instant. If they had gone their separate ways, would there have been a chance one of them would've been spared? He shook his head. It was a thought not to be dissected. The event happened, for if it had not, he would not be chasing such a wonderfully barely dressed lass.

The sweet jiggle of her bottom teased him as she scurried to the table that had been set up near the couch. She suddenly turned to face him, stopping him in his tracks. He grinned in anticipation of the next treat she had planned for his pleasure.

"Sit," she commanded, motioning to the couch.

He did as she requested and plopped down unceremoniously. He couldn't take his eyes off her. Every move she made had his full attention. Donnell relaxed into the corner of the couch closest to the table. Cait lifted the silver lids from the food trays. His mouth watered from the smell wafting in the room. His favorites filled the plates. A thick steak, tiny roasted potatoes and baby carrots lay carefully aligned.

She took a knife and sliced the meat, then turned to feed him. "Open, milord," she said, then licked her lips. "I plan to feed you every bite until your hunger is sated."

He opened his mouth and acted as if he would oblige, then grabbed her wrist when she got near enough to feed him. Her eyebrow arched in question. "It no be food for which I hunger. It be ye, *mi brèagha neamhnaid*."

Before she could stop him, he ran the fingers of his free hand along her channel, skimming any of her essence he could retrieve. He brought those fingers to his lips and sucked them clean. Her eyes widened with desire and her lips parted slightly, letting him know she liked what he did to her.

She leaned close and he thought a kiss would be his reward. But no. "Consider that your appetizer. Now eat, milord." Holding the slice of steak on the fork to his lips, she stated boldly, "You're going to need your strength."

Donnell took the offering. He liked the devilish look in her eyes and was intrigued by the mysterious air about her. It caused his shaft to harden. For the moment, he didn't mind being a pawn in her little game as long it meant he got to be inside her before the break of day. He was hers to tease.

Chapter Seventeen

It was all she could do to concentrate on feeding him. The throb in her mound made it difficult to think of anything but riding him. Now there was an idea. Cait let the smile cross her lips as she turned and rolled the table closer until it was directly beside the couch where she could easily reach it. She laid the fork beside the knife, then moved to stand in front of Donnell.

She placed her hands on his knees, pushing them together, then straddled his thighs. His hands went immediately to her hips, guiding her forward. Cait eased onto her knees on the couch, legs on either side of his, she hovered over him. It still amazed her how quickly he recovered and how many times he could fuck her in a night. She smiled. Tonight she planned to set a record with him, starting now.

Slowly, she lowered until she was fully seated on his shaft. To her, this was heaven having Donnell fill her. It eased her need, if only by a smidgeon. Cait breathed deeply to steady her nerves and focus. She reached for the fork, speared a potato and held it poised to feed him. Gently she rocked her hips and

Donnell smiled, leaning comfortably into the couch.

"Is this the better way to feed you?" she questioned.

"Aye," Donnell answered, then ate the offering. He caressed her breasts through the fine fabric. "These are the part of ye I'd like to have in my mouth instead of food."

He captured a nipple, sucked it into his mouth along with the negligee. The sensation his tongue created rubbing the fabric against her sensitive nub made her shiver. Donnell slowly pumped into her and she nearly caved. It amazed her she was able to gain any control over the situation. She squeezed her knees tightly against his hips.

"Donnell," she gasped, even though she tried to sound stern, "you are not to move. I haven't finished feeding you yet."

"Ye are the only food I want."

Not listening to her, he plowed into her, causing her breasts to bounce in rhythm with his movement. Cait tossed the fork onto the table, grabbed his shoulders for support and rode her man. She had to have him. Though she'd tried her best to extend the tease, she'd fallen to desire and the undeniable need for him. He grabbed the silk ribbon in the crest of her bosom and tugged. The front of the negligee separated and with each bounce of her upon him, her breasts wiggled free of the sheer material.

She kissed him, needing his flavor upon her tongue. He tasted of steak and potato, which made her hungry. In the back of her mind, she realized she hadn't followed her plan. *Bathe him, feed him, fuck him raw until he screams his love for me.* Sensual visions of his lips consuming the slice of steak and the one tiny potato appeared behind her eyes then fizzled out of sight as he speared into her hard and fast. She'd bathed him. She'd sort of fed him and now she rode him.

Convinced she was more or less sticking to her plan, Cait increased her pace, gyrating her hips as he steadily filled her repeatedly. His mouth moved from breast to breast as his hands kneaded her ass, urging her on. Donnell tugged on her nipple and she nearly lost it. Shivers of urgent need shot from her breast straight to her clit, tightening it even more. Her inner walls clenched and there was no controlling her body any further. The orgasm roared through her, drenching him, pulling him in as far as possible.

He twitched inside her. Instantly heated moisture spilled from him, mixing with her juices, filling her, completing her. Cait rocked ever so gently on him before collapsing into his arms. She'd wait all day to be with him. This was bliss.

Several long minutes passed as they leaned into each other in the seated position on the couch until she felt Donnell's arm move. Cait pushed upright, kegeling, not letting him slip free. He brought a fork holding a carrot to her lips.

"I believe we both could use some sustenance." He grinned and Cait shook her head, smiling at him.

"I'm not a big fan of carrots." She wiggled on his lap to emphasize her meaning. "I prefer meat. There's more protein."

Donnell's head fell back as laughter boomed from him. Cait couldn't resist and broke into a bout of laughter as well. She knew he understood the protein expression because they'd had a long discussion on it one day when she'd said something about cock and protein. Once they sobered, she gave him a quick peck on the lips before she stood. "Relax here. I'll be right back."

She hurried into the bathroom, cleaned herself then gathered the cloth and the towel. On the way through the bedroom, she grabbed the wine and glasses. Donnell popped a forkful of steak into his mouth as she entered. She gave him a raised-eyebrow look and playfully stated as she set the wine and glasses on the table, "You couldn't wait for me."

"Nope," he responded, "it has been suggested I shall need my strength this evening. No let it be said a MacKinnon man failed to obey his lady."

Heat filled her chest as she moved to stand between his knees. Gently she clasped him in the cloth and cleaned him. Donnell's attempt to eat stalled as his gaze landed on hers. "Ye keep that up and ye best be ready for another go."

She wagged her eyebrows at him as she dried him with the towel, then tossed it along with the cloth to the floor. "I can go all night. Care to test the theory?"

Donnell grinned and held a fork with a slice of steak toward her. "Aye, *mi brèagha neamhnaid*, I do." He gathered her hand with his free one. "Come sit beside me and let us eat our fill, for it seems we both need to replenish our stamina."

Cait bit the steak from the fork and settled onto the couch. Donnell stood and moved the table in front of the couch, then returned to his place beside her. She'd never been fed before and she had to admit she kind of liked it. Each fed the other until both plates were clean. Cait reached for the wine and filled their glasses. She handed one to Donnell and took the other. She held hers near his and proposed a toast.

"Here's to a very fulfilling night of sex with the man I love." Cait froze. She hadn't meant to admit it to him yet. It slipped.

Their glasses lingered, not touching, separated by a slender gap that seemed a mile wide to her. Cait's heart pounded and the air locked in her lungs. She couldn't look at him. Instead, she focused on the red wine in the glass.

Donnell's warm touch to her chin lifted her face and made her meet his gaze. His stare was unreadable. Oh God, she'd failed. She wanted to run and hide but couldn't. His thumb caressed her trembling lower lip. When Donnell downed his glass without touching it to hers and accepting the toast, it was all she could do not to burst into tears.

He stood and held his hand to her. "Shall we continue this in the bedroom?"

Uncertain what she should do, Cait followed his action, downed her glass and pretended nothing had changed. She took his hand and let him guide her into a standing position. He released her with a gentle shove toward the bedroom. Though her legs were shaky and heavy, she managed to succeed in making it to the bed. Cait turned down the covers.

Donnell walked into the room, carrying the strawberries and cream she'd prepared for dessert. He set them on the nightstand, then turned to face her. Without a word, he kissed her passionately as he guided her onto the bed to lie crossways instead of lengthwise. Her knees were bent comfortably over the bed's edge. He tucked a pillow under her head, then nudged the negligee open as he placed kisses along the center of her body until he reached the apex between her thighs. There he stopped. He stood, staring at her.

"Ye are the most beautiful woman my eyes have ever seen, Cait." His gaze held a mystery she couldn't decipher. It made her tremble inside worried he was unhappy with what she'd said. His tone gave nothing away, no anger or joy. "It be my turn to please ye."

He reached for the thick cream. Her gaze glued to his hands. Steadily he dribbled a line of the fluffy stuff from between her breasts to the top of her slit then returned the bowl to the nightstand. Second, he held the bowl of strawberries. Carefully he created a trail of them in the cream, strategically placing them at precise intervals apart. Once the empty bowl was beside the remaining cream, he lowered to his knees. His height made her easy access in this position. He blew a heated breath along her slit and she shivered in anticipation.

Donnell gave her a swift lick, taking her clit between his lips. Cait gasped. He may not love her but he sure knew how to heat her blood. Moisture instantly pooled within her and he must've sensed it. His finger entered her as he sucked her clit, causing Cait to lift her pelvis, pushing against his face. Donnell nuzzled her back down onto the bed. His darkened, sexy gaze traversed the length of her body to meet her barely opened eyes.

"Do I have your attention, milady?" he questioned.

Cait licked her lips and managed one word, "Aye."

He grinned, then feasted upon her with a passionate abandon that drove her straight into another wrenching orgasm. He didn't stop there. Once he licked her juices clean, he slowly followed the trail he created. The tip of his tongue lapped the cream from the upper edge of her slit, then he devoured the strawberry.

In tortuous slow motion, he licked his way from strawberry to strawberry, leaving a sticky trail behind and setting her insides on fire with a renewed desire for him. He was killing her with every nibble of his teeth to her flesh as he retrieved a strawberry. By the time he hovered over the one between her breasts, Cait could barely breathe. Every ounce of her burned with need. Her nipples were solid, painful peaks aching for his touch. She dripped wanting his cock. She fisted the covers, uncertain if she should touch him.

Donnell lifted the last strawberry and held it mere inches above her mouth. Slowly he lowered it to her lips and she obeyed, taking his offering. She chewed then swallowed. He waited then kissed her. He tasted of strawberries and cream. The head of his shaft bumped against her and she moaned, spreading her legs, hoping he'd ease her desperate need for him to fill her.

Gently he rubbed along her slit, not entering her, simply caressing her, teasing her unmercifully. He nipped her lower lip then held her gaze with his. Pure hunger shone in his eyes. Their faces were mere inches apart.

"Cait, I have never spoken these words to another that I speak to ye now. I love ye, *mi brèagha neamhnaid.* My heart belongs to ye."

He plunged into her, driving his words home. Tears of joy flowed as she held his face in her hands and kissed him. Her fears were lifted with every pump. Cait couldn't stop kissing him as they made love. She wrapped her legs around him, pulling him in deeper with every stroke. Faster, harder, slow and tender, they alternately mixed the rhythm, increasing the pressure within them.

Neither wanted to stop. They'd reach the almost breaking point, then slow the pace, drawing out the lovemaking. She had no clue when or how they maneuvered into the center of the bed but they did. There were no longer boundaries between them as they enjoyed the passions of each other. Lip upon lip, they teased and tasted the other, luxuriating in the flavors.

"Donnell," Cait screamed as she couldn't hold back any longer. The orgasm took her, pulling him over into the wave with her.

Pumping until he was empty, Donnell fell onto her, carefully holding his weight on his forearms so as not to crush her. He placed soft kisses to her closed eyes then whispered in her ear, "I love ye, Cait."

Never had he felt this fulfilled. Lying in her arms made him the happiest and the saddest man in the world. He didn't want to pull from her but was forced to by a sudden sharp pain in his chest. An invisible fist clenched his heart and he feared it would stop beating at any moment. Not wanting her to see the grimace he knew held his face contorted, he eased from the haven of her sheath and lay facedown beside her.

Though it lasted mere seconds, it seemed an eternity before the pain lessened. Cait shifted on the bed beside him. Her whispered words laden with concern eased the knot twisting inside his chest. "Are you all right, Donnell?"

He forced his arms to work and tugged her close, wrapping himself around her. "Aye, *m'gaol*—my love," he replied, doing his best to make his voice sound normal as he swallowed the intensity of the subsiding pain. "Rest. We still have a few hours of night to enjoy each other and I plan to make the most of them."

Cait's tired laugh gave him more pleasure than she'd ever know. Donnell smiled into her hair as she snuggled against him. It would be a while before his shaft would respond for another sample of her beauty, but he fully intended to please her at least once more before the damned curse took him at sunrise.

* * * * *

As the sun threatened their time, Donnell kissed her lips while he lay nestled in her heat. On a heavy sigh, he boasted, "I think that be six if'n my count be right."

Cait stroked his cheek and mimicked him. "Ye be right. Care to try for seven?"

Faint hints of the sun dared to peek through the curtain's edge. Sadly he pulled from her and forced himself from the bed. "As much as I wish to remain buried within the heaven between those magnificent thighs," he said as he motioned toward the window, "the sun rises. Rest and make ready for tonight. I promise we shall break seven."

Cait's wicked grin warmed his heart. She slid from the bed and reached for him. He couldn't resist and took her in his arms for one last kiss that would have to last him throughout the day. When he tried to pull away, she locked her arms around him and refused to let go.

Donnell pried his lips from hers. Panic filled him. "Cait. Ye have to let go. We know not what the curse will do should we be touching when it takes me."

She grinned, released him and marched to the window. She jerked the curtains wide open. Early-morning sunlight spilled into the room. Donnell's jaw dropped. He couldn't believe what he saw. He lifted his hands and stared at them, flexing them into and out of fists. Slowly he lowered his arms and met her excited gaze.

"How?" he asked, confusion riddled his question.

"Love sets the heart free of the curse."

"Love?"

"Aye, love has freed you."

Donnell crossed to Cait and gathered her in his arms. His lips found hers as he spun her around until they landed on the bed. Instantly her legs wrapped around his waist as she teased, "Care to go for seven?"

The End…Until the next brother is found! ☺

Dual Release

ABOUT THE AUTHOR

Tara Nina creates in a variety of ranges from steamy hot to simmering sweet, which includes paranormals, contemporaries, suspense and sci-fi. She's a Southerner living in the northern wilds of New Jersey complete with grown children, two dogs, six turtles and a mountain man for a husband.

She loves to hear from readers so feel free to contact her via email tara@taranina.com

Please don't get discouraged if it takes a little while before she responds. Unfortunately, she hasn't hit the lottery yet and has to work to battle the bills of home ownership. Being a full-time writer is on her bucket list and one day, she hopes to achieve that goal.

Join her Clan MacKinnon Fan Club/Newsletter for updates on what's new and exciting in her world. http://taranina.com/join-the-clan/

Check out her website http://taranina.com

She is also available on the following media outlets:

Facebook: https://www.facebook.com/TaraNinaAuthor

Twitter: https://twitter.com/taranina

Pinterest: https://www.pinterest.com/taranina/

Instagram: https://www.instagram.com/taranina1

Books by Tara Nina

Cursed MacKinnon's series:

Curse of the Gargoyle (book 1)

Eyes of Stone (book 2)

Cursed Laird (book 3)

Haunted Laird (book 4)

All I Want for Christmas is a Marine

Mountain Men: Brothers Dupree ~ Trilogy

Mindwarp

Playing Cowboy

Candygram

Excerpt
Mountain Men
Brothers Dupree
By
Tara Nina

That fucking snow and ice storm couldn't have picked a worse time to roll through the mountains of Montana. Beartooth Mountain and the small town of Red Lodge in particular had been hit hardest. Power and phone lines were down throughout the region. Cell towers were sparse and ineffective. A total whiteout. Emergency crews worked diligently to repair the damage, but it could be weeks. It didn't help her situation that her home was located deep in the woods on the side of the mountain. Desolate to say the least, but private as she and her husband liked it.

Violet sat on the back porch of the old log cabin, wrapped in a blanket and seeking comfort with a steamy mug of cocoa. Her head throbbed from all the tears she'd shed. It'd been eight days since Emmett went missing in the hills of Afghanistan. The storm hit the night after she'd been informed of the accident. This was torture. The not knowing.

This was supposed to be his last tour of duty before being shipped stateside permanently.

The last she'd heard from Emmett, he was boarding a chopper heading to the airport for home. She'd gotten worried when she hadn't spoken with him since. He'd promised to call when he landed back on American soil. She never got that call. When the phone rang at three a.m. on that fateful day, she'd expected to hear Emmett's voice explaining what had delayed him.

"Mrs. Dupree," Captain Erickson had said in a solemn tone. "I'm calling to inform you that your husband, Gunnery Sergeant Dupree, is missing. We are aware he was supposed to arrive home yesterday, and I felt, as his captain and friend, it was my duty to call and keep his family abreast of the situation."

It's a phone call no family member ever wanted to receive. Somehow she'd managed to scrape together enough courage to speak. "Is he dead?"

"We don't know, ma'am."

The captain had said something else, but she'd heard only select words over the fear thrumming through her veins. "Helicopter crashed," "search party," "doing reconnaissance" and then the call ended. It had taken her over an hour to still the tears long enough to call his folks. They'd been so supportive, suggested she stay with them until Emmett was found. But she couldn't do it, couldn't leave the home they'd worked so hard over the past two years renovating, turning into the perfect place for them. It helped knowing his parents were just a ten-minute snowmobile ride away and if she needed to talk, the two-way radio sat on the kitchen counter. Emmett's mother, Rachel, and his father, Dave, touched base with her every few hours or so to make sure she was fine, that the fire burned and the generator ran.

Every afternoon this past week, Emmett's brother, Cash, had swung by on his snowmobile to cart wood from the shed to the indoor bin so she wouldn't have to do the hard work. Today, he'd even suggested they target practice with the rifle, which she'd enjoyed and had done very well because she'd kept picturing the word *Afghanistan* in the bullseye. Violet had been grateful for his help. He'd eased her loneliness a tad. But he wouldn't let her assist with the wood. At least lugging wood would have been strenuous and tiring. Maybe tiring enough she'd get some sleep, but she doubted it.

"Keep your chin up, Violet," Rachel had said during their last two-way chat. "He's coming home. That sand pit over there isn't tough enough to take a Dupree."

Violet wished she held the same positive outlook as Rachel or at least a tenth of her strength and conviction. Emmett had been missing for over forty-eight hours before she'd gotten that call. The day after that, the snow and ice storm hit, taking out all forms of communication with the world outside the mountain and now five days more had passed. On a good day, cell phone and Internet connectivity were iffy. The longer this dragged out, the thinner Violet's nerves stretched.

She leaned into the corner of the porch swing, stretching her legs along the cushioned bench. Taking a long sip of the cocoa, she stared across the snow-covered yard to the woods. Rays from the full moon danced upon the virgin-white surface. If Emmett were home, there'd be one big snow angel out there made just for her, instead of a blank sheet of nothingness. She shivered.

"He's coming home," she whispered, holding the cup in both hands close to her chest. She closed her eyes and struggled to shove away the bad thoughts.

After three tours of duty and twenty years of service, it was time, in her opinion, for Emmett to join the civilian world. She'd met him through her brother, Tim, who owned a bar near the Marine base in Oceanside, California. She could see their meeting clear as day.

She'd sat at the corner of the wooden bar, keeping her brother company between him serving drinks to customers. A trio of guys had walked in and sat at the far end from Violet. One of them in particular had the most amazing brown eyes she'd ever seen. Thick black lashes that would make even a cover model envious. His high-and-tight haircut gave him away as military, quite possibly a Marine since Tim's bar was located within a half a mile of one of their biggest bases. Every time those eyes looked toward her, she couldn't help but blush and look away, embarrassed she'd been caught staring at him. But those eyes kept drawing her back to him.

Violet hadn't come there to pick up anyone, quite the opposite. She'd come to visit her brother to recuperate from having finally ended a bad relationship that had lasted two years too many. When Emmett had walked to her end of the bar, she remembered not being able to breathe and she hadn't been able to do anything but stare at him as he moved toward her, back straight, over six feet tall, broad shoulders and a smile that lit his face and gave him the cutest set of dimples. He'd taken the seat next to her and reached for her hand. She'd liked the way he held it. A gentle strength had oozed from his touch and when he'd spoken, she'd nearly melted like a giddy schoolgirl. That truly was unlike her. She wasn't innocent nor was she a schoolgirl. Nope. She was an educated twenty-seven-year-old woman.

"Hi, I'm Emmett Dupree." His gaze had never left hers. Those eyes had captivated and held her defenseless. "You must be Tim's sister, Violet. He warned us he'd shoot any one of us who made a play on you." He'd leaned closer. The heat of his breath had brushed her cheek as he'd whispered near her ear. "There's something about you that has captured my attention to the point I'm willing to take a bullet just to spend a few moments in time with you."

She'd sat back, putting a bit of space between them, then had placed her palm flat on the center of his chest as she'd leaned forward until their noses had been millimeters apart. Staring into each other's eyes, not blinking, she'd responded, "Marine, that's some pick-up line you've got going there. But I'll let you in on a secret. I've seen Tim shoot.

He couldn't hit the broadside of a barn even if he stood directly in front of it." Then she'd done something she never had before in her life. She kissed a stranger, full on, tongue invasion, war of dominance. And he'd responded. Breathlessly, she'd disengaged and shoved him back. "Game on, soldier. You up for the task?"

He'd grinned from ear-to-ear. "Yes, ma'am. I do believe you've met your match."

They'd started dating, become engaged, and married, knowing they'd found their perfect mates. Violet brushed away the tear that memory caused. Emmett brought out her bold, sexual side and loved every full-figured inch of her. If she even suggested going on a diet, he'd bake her a cherry pie and smother it with ice cream. He loved her just the way she was built. Said he liked his wife soft, plump and a bit on the sturdy side. Made for good loving for a man his size, six-foot-five and two hundred twenty-five pounds of muscle.

She pushed the swing with her foot, making it rock. God, she missed him and wanted him home. When he'd shipped out this last time, she'd moved their stuff to the log cabin and had worked furiously to make it their own. Painting, decorating and unpacking. She looked at the undecorated Christmas tree standing in the corner by the front window, waiting for Emmett to help her turn it into something beautiful.

This was supposed to be his homecoming. He'd volunteered to spend the last five months of his career as a Marine overseas in Afghanistan, training a group for their first tour of duty. Since he'd already been there twice, he knew the ins and outs of dealing with the locals, the terrain, the sudden sandstorms, and other shit that happened. He'd felt it was his duty to acclimate the others. He'd said it would be a piece of cake, in for five months and then home for good. Discharged. Retired from the military.

Though she'd only been a part of his life for the last four years, she knew he'd given plenty to the Corps, which made her beam with pride. He was the perfect Marine. Thinking of him in his dress blues at their wedding brought a smile to her lips. He'd stood ramrod straight, staring at her and smiling broadly, causing his dimples to appear even deeper when her daddy had walked her down the aisle.

"My beautiful Violet. On this day, you are making me the happiest man in the world by becoming my wife." The memory of his vows whispered through her ears. *"I hand my heart to you. Please don't drop it."*

That moment of happiness dissipated as the wind whistled through the trees. Violet tucked the blanket closer, knowing she should go inside before she caught a chill. She wasn't ready to face the emptiness of their bedroom and an oversized king mattress that swallowed her without him.

Violet prayed for Emmett's safe return. She wanted her husband home for good. No one outside of the service truly understood the anguish a military wife and family went through each time a deployment occurred. The gnawing sensation that brewed in the pit of one's stomach, sleepless nights that were endless with a whole lot of prayers spoken for their safety. Being proud of them for serving only went so far in soothing the loneliness and living in fear, not knowing if they'd return in a box or on their own accord.

If she heard one more time that absence made the heart grow fonder, she'd yank the throat from the next person to say it. She'd skipped the last two Sunday services because she was so sick of hearing it, even though she knew the ladies of the women's Bible group meant well. And then there was that odd man, Phil Stokes. It seemed he just happened to run into her everywhere she went in town. Didn't matter what day of the week or the time, he simply appeared, which had started giving her the creeps. Was he stalking her? He couldn't offer enough help to her. It had gotten to the point she was running out of polite ways to say *no thank you*.

A deep void filled her soul with Emmett's disappearance that was worse than living alone through this last deployment. Her heart had been ripped down its middle, leaving a raw open gash in its place. He was on his way home. That helicopter was transporting him to the flight that would be the first in a long journey homeward bound. It never made it. She bit her lip.

Stop thinking about it. He's coming home.

Silence surrounded her with the exception of the low hum from the gas-powered generator located in the garage. It sat under the circuit box inside the first bay door closest to the house. The day before the storm, her father-in-law had been by and made sure the fifty-five gallon upright gas container with an easy-to-use pump handle was completely filled and positioned within reach of the generator. She kept the garage door cracked just a tiny bit to let the fumes escape, but not opened enough for any critters to get in. Not that any were moving around in the six feet of snow that had been dumped by the storm. Usually she enjoyed the snow. Not now, not when she was left without any way to receive word about Emmett.

Maybe not hearing was best. Tomorrow would be Christmas Eve. This was to be their first Christmas spent in their house as civilians. Emmett's discharge papers had been written and given to him the day before he stepped on that flight home. What he'd sworn was a simple training mission had turned into a full-blown nightmare. She rolled her head against the back of the swing and caught sight of something moving fast. She sat upright, stood and moved to the porch railing, chin tilted, watching the tiny twinkle glide across the clear night sky.

Violet closed her eyes and made a wish on that shooting star.

Dual Release